I0647502

POPULAR PUBLICATIONS  FACSIMILE EDITIONS

Shock #3
(July 1948)

Shock was launched in 1948 by Popular Publications as a companion magazine to its primary detective pulps, *Dime Detective* and *Black Mask*, concentrating on weird-mystery stories. The third issue contains stories by Frederick C. Davis, Theodore Sturgeon, and John D. MacDonald.

Authors:

Frederick C. Davis, Scott O'Hara, John Bender, Theodore Surgeon, John D. MacDonald, Bruce Cassidy, Marian O'Hearn

Illustrators:

Everett Raymond Kinstler, Monroe Eisenberg

NOTE: We have attempted to restore the original page scans in this facsimile in order to provide an enjoyable reading experience. However, in some cases there can be text loss due to damage to the original pulp, tight bindings, or other reasons.

15¢ THE **NEW MYSTERY** MAGAZINE

SHOCK

Volume 1 July, 1948 Number 3

The next issue will be out August 4th.

Published bi-monthly by New Publications, Inc., at 2256 Grove Street, Chicago 16, Illinois. Editorial and Executive Offices, 210 East 43rd Street, New York 17, N. Y. Henry Steeger, President and Secretary, Harold S. Goldsmith, Vice President and Treasurer. Entered as second-class matter January 14, 1948, at the post office at Chicago, Illinois, under the Act of March 3, 1879. Copyright, 1948, by New Publications, Inc. This issue is published simultaneously in the Dominion of Canada. Copyright under International Copyright Convention and Pan-American Copyright Conventions. All rights reserved, including the right of reproduction, in whole or in part, in any form. Single copy, 15c. Annual subscription price for U.S.A., its possessions and Canada, 90c; other countries 25c additional. All correspondence relating to this publication should be addressed to 2256 Grove Street, Chicago 16, Illinois, or 210 East 43rd Street, New York 17, N. Y. When submitting manuscripts, enclose stamped self-addressed envelope for their return if found unavailable. Care will be exercised in the handling of unsolicited manuscripts, but no responsibility for their return is assumed. Any resemblance between any character appearing in fictional matter, and any person living or dead, is entirely coincidental and unintentional. Printed in U.S.A.

I'll Marry
a Killer!

She said, "Quite an ungraceful rat, aren't you, my precious?"

CHAPTER ONE

Blind Date With Death

*H*ER heart-beat was wild. I felt the swift surging of it as she lay there with her blue-green eyes gazing up, wide and soft and yielding.

"Darling," I whispered. "Darling...."
She didn't speak. Her red lips were

Startling Suspense Novel

By Frederick C. Davis

Her lips still warm from my kiss, my lovely bride-to-be stole furtively into the night—a bewitching, vibrant she-devil whose rendezvous was . . . murder.

ported and trembling on silence. Just her fast breath came from them, her little jerky pulled-in sobs.

"Darling," I whispered. "This is it. Not the way we expected—but this is it. . . ."

Darkness all around. It closed us in together. And it was silent except for the quick sibilance on her moist red lips and the pounding of her pulse like a savage tom-tom.

Holding her close, feeling her breath warm on my face, I looked into the fog outside the window. Coiling and writhing as if with a sinuous life of its own, the fog seemed to be standing watch in the street for us. It seemed to raise a dark hand and beckon; to say, "Come on now. Get going while you've still got the chance. Your chance in a million with her—your last chance for ever. . . ."

I lifted her in my arms, very gently. Her eyes were pleading and her breath breaking in wordless sobs and her heartbeat wildly swift as I carried her through the door, out into a secret world where the fog would guard and cloak us.

The blood on her lips was only a fleck . . .

Cyn didn't know I was watching her that night—it was only two nights ago—when she slipped out of the house with such quiet grace . . . and such heart-chilling stealth.

She eased out of the door on the driveway side. For half a moment she poised there, listening, making sure she had succeeded in sneaking this far without discovery.

A lovely figure she was, suspended in motion in the emerald-green glow radiating from the bay window of her father's study. Her hair, glistening shoulder-length, was almost the yellow of daisies. She held her short fox jacket closed, one of her hands at her throat, her long scarlet-tipped fingers still, and her other hand thrust out of sight under the fur. Her lips shone as she moistened them and glanced back at her room upstairs, where the windows still glowed a cozy, deceitful pink.

This girl at the door was Miss Cynthia Parke, twenty-two years old and fully of age. Socially she was top drawer. Her father, Judge Spencer Parke, was about to enter into a well-earned retirement, complete with testimonial dinner. He was also a very rich man, and Cyn was in line to inherit all his wealth, including the Parke estate on Sycamore Boulevard—this same mansion from which she was sneaking tonight without his knowledge.

Unquestionably one of the city's classiest young women, Cynthia Parke; and in my estimation unquestionably its most desirable. During the past weeks congratulations had swarmed upon me. Our engagement had been formally announced. In only a few more weeks Cynthia and I were to be married—a huge church wedding, of course, with all the fanciest trimmings appropriate to the nuptials of our local princess.

BUT tonight Cyn was slipping out of her own home after having complained prettily to her fiancé, "You won't mind letting the invitation list go another night, will you, Vince, darling? I think I'd really better turn in right now and get rid of this perfectly lousy headache."

"Sure I mind losing this evening with you, Cyn," I had said. "But hop right into bed. I'll phone a little later to see how you're coming along."

"Oh, please don't phone tonight, Vince, darling! I—I expect to drop right off to sleep, I'm so terribly tired. Call me in the morning instead. Late—about noon, darling."

She'd said that a little too fast, I'd thought—a little too anxiously.

That had been only half an hour ago. Being of a slightly suspicious nature—and this wasn't the first time I had felt twinges about Cyn, either—I had spent that half hour keeping out of sight in the shadow behind the garage.

This was, of course, no way to treat a lovely fiancée, and I was filled with self-censure as I gazed up at the lights of Cyn's bedroom. I was a heel, spying on her like this, I kept telling myself. I didn't deserve her.

Then the side door of the house had stealthily opened and Cyn had sidled out. She seemed ethereally lovely as she paused there in the dim green light, her eyes glittering with her secret purpose. A hidden, audacious purpose that I couldn't guess. Not entirely.

She started along the driveway on her glimmering sandals and scarlet-tipped toes—straight toward the garage, one of her hands still hidden inside her fox jacket.

I drew back into the shadow behind the garage, sucking in my breath, feeling electrically Cyn's nearness. She could always do that to me—throw a galvanic charge into me with a glance, a flicker of a smile, a single light touch. So I felt her closeness as she came through the early night. And I felt a little sick at heart also when I discovered how neatly she had planned it.

She had brought her convertible in from the rear gate earlier this evening and had left it there in the parking space. Now she simply eased behind the wheel and quietly released the hand-brake. The slope of the driveway started the car drifting as soundlessly as a canoe on a millpond. It passed the house in its silk-smooth way, then veered into the street. A brief purr of the starter, unnoticeable inside the judge's study, and Cyn was on her way.

Dodging along the driveway, I took a quick glance inside the judge's windows. A trim, white-headed man, he was reading in the light of a fine old student lamp,

oblivious to her slick little piece of trickery.

When I reached the driveway, Cyn's car was already several blocks away. I hustled around the corner, where I had left my own sedan instead of heading back to my apartment, as Cyn had expected me to do. A fine foundation, this, for a lasting marriage, I thought sourly—the bride off on a secret excursion to parts unknown with the groom hot on her trail. But I had to have the answer—and much better early than late.

Veering my sedan past the corner, I braked sharply. I had momentarily forgotten the obstruction in the street. Leaving only a single traffic lane, a deep excavation cut across it, exposing pipes and conduits eight or ten feet below. I skirted past the wooden horses with their hanging lanterns, hastening to follow the crimson glimmer that marked the course of Cyn's car.

Then the hairs on the back of my neck began to crawl. Tailing Cyn, I felt an uncanny sensation warning me that I myself was being tailed.

The rear-view mirror showed me nothing. Twisting around to peer backward, I still saw nothing. No car bearing after me anywhere in the broad, open street. Yet, as I followed the floating scarlet star of Cyn's tail-lights, I couldn't shake off the chilling feeling that somehow *both* of us were being relentlessly dogged.

IT WAS sparkling clear that evening. Stars glittered like points of clean new steel. The twin gleams of Cyn's car stayed a bright red on the road ahead, vivid and taunting.

She had led me outside the city, past farms and orchards. I was still jockeying to keep her in sight when the dash clock reminded me it was just two hours since she had given me a goodnight kiss and had gone upstairs.

Her father had listened for her bedroom door to close. Then he had taken my arm in a manner of the friendliest confidence and had said quietly, "Vince, my boy, tell me frankly—"

Pausing there, Judge Spencer Parke stood tall and straight. "Vince, we've been fine friends for a long time now. We can speak frankly to each other. Have you noticed—well, how jumpy Cynthia has been this past week or so? Jumpy as a cat!"

"Cyn's very high-strung, Spencer—she's a thoroughbred," I reminded him. "With the extra strain on the wedding piling up—"

"There must be more than that behind Cynthia's nervousness." Judge Parke fixed me with his sensitive blue eyes. "I've noticed you watching Cynthia, my boy, puzzling over her agitation just as I have. She's on edge—full of anxiety about something she's keeping to herself."

Watching him, and keeping my own thoughts to myself as closely as Cyn was keeping hers, I asked, "Can you explain it, Spencer?"

A frown put dark lines in his fine, high forehead. "Part of it rises out of her nature. This isn't the first time Cynthia has needed watching. In fact, she has needed it all her life.

I said: "There's fire in her, all right. Enough to make her too hot to handle sometimes?"

His glance was keen. "Born in her, Vince. Fire straight out of her mother's veins. You never knew Cynthia's mother; she died too long ago. Brazilian and Spanish. Latin blood with a fever in it. High-tempered. Hair-trigger. I've seen young women of that sort brought before my bench. Prisoners—charged with homicide." He squared his shoulders. "Vince, that girl has a certain wildness in her that rages up at times. . . ."

Judge Parke turned his clear blue eyes on me. "I must confess I don't know my daughter too well. She may have—well, done things; wild, impulsive things

which I've never heard about. And I don't want to hear about them, now or ever. All I can say, Vince, is that I hope something of this sort is not causing the agitation and fever I have felt in Cynthia lately."

It was a jolt, despite the judge's consideration for my feelings—this suggestion that Cyn, even while arranging for her wedding to me, might be relaxing from the strain by quietly playing around with some other guy in her off moments. But I had to recognize, even so, that the notion wasn't entirely unthought-of on my part. Not that I had dreamed up the suspicions, either; I had reasons which I could not ignore entirely.

But I managed to keep my voice steady as I asked, "Since we're talking man-to-man, Spencer—have you anything specific behind that suggestion?"

He hesitated, pursing his lips. "No-o, Vince. I simply feel we should keep an eye on Cynthia and not let her—well, overstrain herself. That's all, my boy."

I could have added a few details, perhaps a few the judge himself had not noticed.

FOR example, how drained of energy Cyn had seemed several times recently—as if she had had no sleep at all the previous night, although she had apparently gone up to her bedroom at the usual time. A certain guilty furtiveness in her manner—her quick, watchful glances, her sudden alarmed tensions. Once, joining her and the judge for Sunday breakfast at her home, I had seen something she hadn't noticed herself—still-damp mud on her spike heels. There had been, of course, no mud on these same shoes when she had kissed me good-night at the door, when I had left her the previous midnight.

Also, only a few days ago a gossip-loving twerp named Bunny Cosford had stopped at our table while we were having lunch at the University Club. He had said in silly glee, "So, Cyn, my sweet, you're the kind who leaves a friend high and dry—and at such an ungodly hour, too! Four a.m., no less."

Cyn had said quickly, giving him a freezing frown, "Are you by any chance being hilarious, Bunny? Somehow I miss the point of your comedy."

"You know perfectly well what I mean, dearie. It was four a.m. this morning, down at Dock and Warehouse Streets— horrible neighborhood—where my car had just run out of gas on my way back from the Hillbilly Club. I was trying desperately to flag a ride home when you went zipping right past me in that ducky new scooter of yours. Where on earth had you been at such a unholy hour, dear? And alone, too!"

"Oh, go away," Cyn had said sharply. "You were drunk, disorderly and having hallucinations. At four this morning I was in bed at home. Go away, I said, Bunny, you half-witted, drooling fool! And shut up!"

The lash of her words hit with a spiteful sting. Bunny retorted, "Hmmm. So sorry. My mistake, dumpling," and went stumbling off, sneering, to another table of friends.

I said, laughing and reaching for Cyn's hand, "Next time he won't jump to any such sappy conclusions about you, like that one, sugar."

But Cyn's hand had been icy-cold and she had secretly terrified, with her lips livid and her cheeks flaming. And she had said, "Stupid little driveler!" with blistering heat rather than the bantering laugh that such a trivial incident would have called for—*if Bunny had not really seen her.*

But I said nothing of this to Judge Parke. I had simply begun then and there keeping a little closer eye than usual on this luscious lass. Surreptitiously at first, from a dark nook behind the garage; now

from behind the wheel of my car as I trailed hers out into the deepening darkness behind the city's fast-disappearing lights. . . .

Had she noticed that she was being followed? If so, she wasn't letting it panic her. She just kept tooling her classy convertible through the darkness at a fast, even clip. Her smooth speed said she knew exactly where she was going and why—which was more than I could guess so far.

Suddenly Cyn swung her car past a fork. Picking up silken speed, she swerved in the direction of a pointer reading *Laurel Bay.*

This move told me at last just where she had been heading from the first. At Laurel Bay, still a sparsely settled spot, Judge Parke owned a beach cottage. It was an idyllic spot in midsummer; but this late in the season, when the winds off the salt marshes blew raw, that whole rough-swept region would be bleak and deserted.

I shivered and thought it was a special date indeed that my bride-to-be was heading for.

The instant Cyn veered into the fork to Laurel Bay, I stopped on the sandy shoulder of the road, far back, and cut all the switches. For miles ahead the road reached through low undulating dunes. From here, where I sat with the taste of brass in my mouth, I would be able to see Cyn's car gliding every foot of the way to her destination. And to a rendezvous as well?

To some other man who was waiting for her there? I couldn't know that. All I could do at this sour-mouthed moment was sit there in the cold salt darkness, with narrowed eyes following Cyn the whole way until she reached the distant cottage.

There she stopped, and her car lights— the only glimmer in that secluded cranny of the night—vanished.

CHAPTER TWO

Sweet—and Satanic

THE blood on her lips had been no more than a fleck—but now another drop had crept out, making a thin scarlet line wavering slowly toward a dark bruise on her chin.

I held her close as I carried her and said softly, "This is it, my beautiful. We can't get away from it now. It's a one-time thing. We can never escape it now—at least never in this world."

The fog was our accomplice, our sentry. It watched over us and hid us as I carried her along that murky street, cloaking us in silence. There was not a sound except my own footsteps, and the spasmodic intake of her breath.

The trickle of blood on her bruise-blackened chin grew longer as our time grew shorter. Shorter moment by moment as I carried her through the evil fog. . . .

Using Cyn's own tactics as an example, I started the motor again and, with my head lamps out, swung into the fork of the road in the direction of Laurel Bay. Playing it carefully, I would be able to roll up close to the Parke cottage with hardly a sound signaling my approach.

Letting the car crawl along the sandy ruts in the night, I watched the spot where the cottage sat. It stayed dark. Whatever Cyn might be doing in there, she wasn't using a light.

A quarter-mile this side of the dark cottage sat a neighbor's cedar bungalow. A pull on the wheel turned my car off the road and into its driveway. Sliding out, I looked across the sea-grassed hillocks. The Parke cottage sat near now, silhouetted against the glimmer of the water beyond, still with every window lightless.

"Dock and Warehouse Streets," Bunny had said. A grimy corner in a section of factories crowding against slum tene-

ments. So what could it have to do with this costly sea-view cottage on exclusive Laurel Point, two hours' drive away?

Waves lapped on the beach as if licking their chops over a juicy morsel, and their sound in the bay was a derisive chuckling. At first I couldn't spot Cyn's car, but soon a gleam of starlight revealed it behind a screen of scrub pine, where no chance passerby was likely to notice it.

I hesitated, cold with the raw night wind and the dread of what might be happening behind those dark windows. But what the hell! So long as I had set out, as no true gentleman would, to get the goods on my lovely fiancée, I'd better do a thorough job, hadn't I?

I took a flashlight from the glove compartment, turned to the road as the quietest way of scouting across to the cottage —and stopped, full of a bristling sense of alarm.

There had been a sound, not from the cottage but from behind me—from my own car.

Flashlight in hand, I faded down to a crouch against a fat, burlap-wrapped box-wood. Something had moved but I couldn't see what it was; and for another tight moment nothing stirred. Then I saw the black trunk-lid lifting.

In frozen amazement I saw the lid swing up, the compartment gape open. Then something was crawling out of it.

The figure straightened itself into that of a man—a small one. He stood there stiffened into a stooped position by his long cramped ride in the trunk. He peered around like an animal wakening to a hunger for prey.

NOW I could understand why I'd felt so mysteriously dogged. I hadn't been followed, exactly; instead, I had unwittingly carted this small shadow right along with me.

Way back there on Sycamore Boulevard he must have guessed my next move even before I'd made it. He must have spotted me in the act of parking just around the corner from the Parke home and skirting back on foot; must have crawled into the rear of my car just half a moment before I had started tooling it after Cyn's.

But why? And who was he? I couldn't recognize him as he stood hunch-shouldered there, getting his joints loosened before sneaking into his next move.

His next move was to prowl toward the road in the direction he knew I had gone.

As he passed the box-bush, I sprang. I caught him by surprise from behind, with an arm hooked hard under his chin. He let out a squeaky gasp, flopping about like a hooked fish in a frantic attempt to escape. Using the flashlight, my only weapon, I slugged him once to discourage that and to keep him from making any noise that might tip Cyn off. I had to bat his skull three times, each time a little more persuasively, before he decided to see it my way.

He went limp. I found myself breathing hard and reflecting that if ever I decided to stop being a respectable young lawyer with a promising political future, I might not do too badly as a thug.

Slightly surprised to find the flashlight still working, I turned it into the man's scared, squinting eyes. Then I did recognize him—with an icy shock. He was Vic Dixon. And Vic Dixon was the *Press's* favorite performer, the top special reporter on their city staff.

He peered up at me with tears of pain in his small, black-button eyes. "Take it a little easier, Mr. Reece. You can hurt a man doing that. You wouldn't like to see my paper front-paging you for roughing up its pet newsman, would you?"

"I don't like the way your paper assigns its chief snooper to smelling around after me like this, Dixon," I said, carefully avoiding any mention of Cyn. "I could raise a bit of a stink about that."

"This is no assignment, brother," Dixon answered, short of breath. "It's my own idea. Once in a while I get an idea like this one. A really hot hunch. A real sizzler."

It was a veiled threat that told me nothing, and Dixon wasn't likely to do much explaining so long as I kept him pinned down in the gravel with a knee on his chest. Besides, Dixon's unaccountable interest in the situation had jockeyed me into a damned peculiar and ticklish spot. Until this moment I had been edging into a private showdown with Cyn. Now, suddenly, I found myself forced to protect her from this conscienceless Paul Pry.

I pulled him to a standing position, keeping one hand on his collar and the other twisted hard around the light. He put on a wry smile that was half sneer. His sly beady eyes estimated me as an adversary.

"Convenient, Mr. Reece, your trunk lock being broken. Made it a little easier for me tonight." He added, lips twisting with insinuation, "This thing's been tough on me, you know—it's costing me a lot of sleep."

"Never mind the cryptic hints, Dixon," I said. "You're in trouble. Start talking your way out of it if you can."

"*I'm* in trouble?" he retorted in his thin voice. Then, going off on an evasive tangent, "Listen, Mr. Reece. I don't blame you for socking me. In your shoes I'd feel plenty jittery, too—anxious as hell to keep this business under wraps. It's going to be tough enough on a right guy like you, Mr. Reece, without you getting mixed up in it any deeper. So I'm giving you a chance to backtrack, and this is it. Go on, Mr. Reece, take your car right now. Clear the hell out of here and leave the rest of this rat-race to me."

"That's really very damned nice of you," I said, "but I'm staying. Never mind the innuendo. Give it to me straight—your cute reason for hiding away in my car."

Frowning, he peered across at the Parke cottage. The glint in his squinting eyes told me he knew Cyn was there. It would be a waste of time trying to tell him different. I'd damned well better face the fact—this slinking little news-hound knew more about her, somehow, than I did.

He looked back, lifting his sly black eyes to mine with a cynical shrug. "Do you really need to be told, Mr. Reece? If so, there's not enough time to do it right now. Let me refer you to tomorrow's *Press*. Meanwhile I might mention one angle. Tonight's the first night you tailed her around, but I started it three nights ago. On a hunch. A newsman's hunch. One of the kind that the instant it hits you you know it's got to be right. It hasn't led me much of anywhere until now. But now I've got the feeling that tonight's the payoff."

"Talk sense!" I tightened my grip on his collar. "What the hell are you driving at?"

Somehow this strange, slick-witted little guy wasn't resentful of the manhandling I'd given him. He really wasn't. On the contrary, he seemed to feel sorry for me.

"Look, Mr. Reece. You don't want to be in on the rest of what's going to happen tonight. Take if from me, you don't. It'll be tough enough when the news hits you second-hand. So head back for the city right now and wait for it, will you, as a big favor to yourself?"

"No."

I SEARCHED his anxiety-pinched face and he went on rapidly, keeping his voice down as he pleaded. "Why sucker yourself into such a mess, Mr. Reece? You're on the way up now, a bright young man with a bright future. I know it's in the cards for you to get elected our next district attorney. With Judge Parke's backing you'll win it in a walk. So don't be a chump—keep your chances good."

"Your concern for my future is really touching."

My sarcasm didn't stop him. "This won't hurt your chances as long as you stay on the outside, but try to take hold of it and it'll pull you down. I'm telling you. Besides, the judge is going to need you right there at his side when this big stink lets loose. You don't realize how rough it's going to be on him. They're trapped here. There's only one way out of this setup and the cops will close in as soon as I get word back. They'll be cornered in there together."

"Trapped? Cornered together? Who? Damn you, *who?*"

The shaking I gave him rattled his teeth but didn't loosen his tongue. He took it without a whine.

"See for yourself, then, if you insist. You won't have to wait long. I'll break it right now—and it will be a bigger story with you right in the middle of it, chump, because you wouldn't take my advice for your own good."

He turned away, evidently intending to break into one of the nearby beach-houses on the chance of finding a usable phone. His purpose, just as plainly, was to call in the police. In a way which was less clear to me than to him, this was a matter of crime; it would break a scandal wide open. And there was only one thing for me to do about it.

No matter how deftly Cyn might be two-timing me, I couldn't let Dixon splash it out in headlines. I couldn't let him hurt my friend the judge, nor would I welcome any sabotage on my own career. He had to be stopped. Cyn had to be given time enough to clear out of her dead-end rendezvous.

That's why I jumped Vic Dixon a second time—from behind again—with no punches pulled.

He whirled away as I snatched at him and ducked under a smashing blow of my flashlight. Its glass lens scattered in shards. He came at me then with a cornered rat's viciousness—teeth bared, springing for my throat. His nails dug deep for my windpipe. I kept smashing at him with the light and my free fist, and we went down together, rolling.

He was squirming under me when he snapped his knees up in a powerful kick. His second kick sent his pointed shoes driving into my face. I reeled back, blinded and sprawling, and when I could lift my head I saw Dixon hustling to verify his filthy hunch.

He was stumbling across the dunes toward the Parke cottage. I pulled myself up and started after him, reeling like a drunk. I was still twenty yards away when he reached the door.

His hands clenched the knob and he was startled to a moment's standstill. Having expected to find the door bolted, he was amazed to find that he could twist the knob and simply push it open. In a frenzy to keep out of my reach and at the same time to pin down his front-page dirt, he thrust it wide and sidled inside.

The door had not yet begun to close behind him when the shots blasted out.

Three shots in swift succession. The reports seemed tremendous bursts in the stillness, but they vanished instantly without even an echo.

I stumbled closer to the open door. Now a steady light had appeared—the shaft of a flashlight aimed from inside the room. It shone down on Vic Dixon as he lay there on the floor just inside the door. Three holes in his belly were leaking blood.

The light was gripped in one of Cynthia Parke's hands, and in the other she clenched the automatic. And both those fine, delicate, patrician hands of hers were as steady as the bony pointing finger of Death.

A very effective job of murder, this—by my tender bride-to-be.

Lying there inert with the blood seeping out of him, Vic Dixon looked as dead as he would ever get—but he wasn't quite dead enough to suit Cyn in her fury. Suddenly the gun in her hand let out its shattering fire again. Twice. With her face strained into lines of sheerest hatred and her fine teeth gleaming in the oval of her tight-pulled lips, she stepped closer to send two more bullets smashing squarely into the hollow of the corpse's gaping mouth.

CHAPTER THREE

Betrothed to Murder

*O*UR TIME *together was already growing heart-breakingly short when I found her car sitting empty in the gray void. She knew, as certainly as I did, where we must go from here. There was only one ending now. This was a one-way passage; it had begun with hot blood and murder and it was steering straight and fast for its final ending.*

As gently as possible I lifted her into the car and put her on the seat. There, with a vibrant impulse, she stirred. Her hand closed hot and tight on mine and she whispered, "Lee . . . Lee!"

My name—the name of her husband-to-be—was Vincent Reece.

She sobbed and clung to me. "My darling—Lee . . ."

After blasting out those last two shots she stood still, her fine face strained with sharpest malice as she spat out, "Foul little spying weasel! Now you're out of my way!"

In the consuming heat of her rage she hadn't so far seen me. She had been so intent, so all-absorbed in the fury of killing Vic Dixon that she hadn't had an instant's thought for anything else. It was as if she had been waiting with a gambler's feverish hope and a hunter's sharp eye for the instant when Dixon would step up to get the life ripped out of him by her storming bullets.

Then she sensed discovery. Her eyes flashed into a swift search. She snapped the beam of her light into my face. I heard her moan at the sight of me.

"Vince!"

The incredulous tone in her ragged voice showed that I was completely unexpected here. She had been counting on someone to come to that dark door about now—but not me.

She stiffened as I stepped through the door, across Dixon's lifeless body, toward her. Then she dropped the light. It rolled on the floor, still burning, and in its shine I saw a subtle, amazing change transform her.

During these few explosive moments she had been a living fury—a girl I had never seen before, one with deadly malevolence glittering in her eyes, her mouth thinned to a line of cruelty, a vicious female with no mercy in her. But in a twinkling she was again the Cynthia I knew—the sensitive thoroughbred—so lovely as she stood there with her lips parted in dismay, a yellow tendril of her hair dangling before one widened eye.

"Vince!" she gasped. "Darling! My Lord, Vince, what have I done?"

"You've murdered a man," I choked. It was all I could say.

She gazed at me with tears beginning to glimmer in her blue-green eyes—such innocent-seeming eyes—and her trembling red lips couldn't form a word.

Unconsciously she had slid her weapon back inside her fox jacket, the same place where she had concealed it when sneaking out of her home. I reached, closed my hand over it, brought it out—and recognized it with a cutting chill.

I had seen it before. It was the registered property of Cyn's father. She had not merely murdered a newsman whose death was hardly likely to be shrugged off—she had done it with Judge Parke's gun!

Suddenly realizing it herself, she flung herself against me, arms tight around me and sobbed, "Oh, Lord, Vince! I had to. The stinking little rat was forcing me to it!"

I knew then—when she clenched herself to me so pleadingly—I would never willingly lose her. Only the devil himself knew what kind of woman Cyn really was. But she had captured me, clinched me as hers long ago—and I would fight Satan himself to keep her.

"LISTEN to me, Cyn," I whispered through her hair. "Try to realize what you've done. You've killed a man. Here, in your father's beach house. With your father's gun. In your fiancé's presence—practically before my eyes. You understand all that?"

She murmured, holding me more tightly, "Help me, darling. I need you so terribly now. Help me, darling."

"Maybe there's a chance. At least nobody else dreams it's happened—so far. You did pick a fine, lonely place to do it, anyhow. Why did you come here, Cyn? Why have you been slipping out of the house every night? Where have you been going—who have you been seeing? I've got to know these things before I can figure a way out of it for you. Spill it, Cyn!"

Her arms loosened. She passed a hand across her eyes, swaying a little. "I—I can't think, Vince. My mind won't work. I feel so—so weak, so dizzy."

Suddenly—and in a manner that wasn't exactly weak or confused either—she snatched the automatic from my hand. Wildness flashed in her eyes again as she whirled away from me. Before I would reach for her, she had broken into a fleet run. Her slender angles twinkled as she sprang across her victim's body and out the door.

When I reached the walk, she was gone in the darkness. A sudden smooth roar of power surged up behind the clump of scrub pine. Her car spurted out of its hiding place, forcing me to leap aside to avoid being swiped. She switched on the lights as she veered again into the road and pressed it to a fast clip.

My first impulse—to scramble into my own car and chase her down—was better forgotten. I had a more important and more pressing assignment than that.

The waves lapped on the beach as if licking their chops over a succulent tidbit of gossip, and the bay was full of their derisive chuckling as I turned back to the murder victim that my bride had left here for me to handle somehow.

*   *   *

Stepping into the cottage over Vic Dixon's corpse, I listened for a second presence somewhere inside. I heard nothing. Dixon stayed just as dead and I found no hint of anyone whom Cyn might have come here to meet.

Picking up the flashlight, I went from one door to another, probing into each room. Everything was in apple-pie order, just as it was left when the cottage was shuttered up for the winter.

There wasn't a suspicious sign anywhere, even in the living room where Cyn had waited in the dark with the judge's gun. The one ashtray on the table contained a few butts, but all of them were touched with Cyn's lip-rouge. She had felt for and brought out a pinch-bottle of scotch from the cupboard, but there was only one shot-glass on the table—she had taken it straight—its rim also carmined by her lips.

No one had been waiting here for Cyn. She had not driven out to this remote cottage to keep a clandestine date with some unknown man. Why, then, had she come—bringing with her such hatred of Vic Dixon that she had blown the life out of him the instant he had stepped in sight?

I could see part of an answer. Cyn had probably tumbled to the fact that tenacious little Dixon was shadowing her everywhere, making himself an unshakable danger to her. So, driven by a desperate need to get rid of him, she had deliberately led him into this murder-trap detour.

If so, it had served her purpose with deadly neatness. He had let her pull off an expert job of luring him to a deserted spot where no one could ever hear the shots. And he definitely wouldn't be tailing her around any more.

I went over to the poor dead little guy who had sneak-played himself right out of this life. It was my turn now to feel sorry for a chump as I went through his pockets. Blood had soaked into several of them; my fingers came out red. Other than his blood, I found nothing of significance except possibly a copy of the latest *Press*.

HE HAD been carrying it folded in a side pocket of his coat. All the local items on the front page were routine except one story to the effect that the police believed they had traced a certain wanted citizen named Shannon to Toledo. Formerly the Mr. Big of several gambling joints downtown, Shannon was a fugitive from a murder rap. His arrest, several states away, was expected hourly, Chief Boshall had announced.

I knew of only the slimmest connection between Shannon and Cyn—I had introduced her to him at one of his lavish cocktail parties eight or nine months ago. That was all.

Including even this, Dixon dead was no more enlightening than he had been when alive. He had been smelling out a sensational splash of some kind, but I had still to learn exactly how it involved the fragile and glamorous Miss Cynthia Parke.

I replaced the scotch bottle in the cupboard and wiped the shot-glass clean. I emptied the crimson-stained butts into a wastebasket and pocketed Cyn's abandoned flashlight. Rolling Dixon halfway over, I made sure, gratefully, that the floor under him would not need mopping. All I had left to do now was arrange matters so that Dixon would not still be here when Judge Parke came to open up the place next spring.

As to the disposal of her victim's body, my betrothed hadn't stayed long enough to tell me what she might have planned to do about it. She had left that little detail to the devices of her ever-devoted fiancé.

I hooked my fingers into the corpse's collar and dragged . . .

When I curbed my car at a safe distance back from the corner of Sycamore Boulevard, it was well past midnight. Hardly a glow was to be seen in this top-drawer neighborhood. Everybody was decently asleep; everything was tranquilly dark and very, very respectable.

Easing out of the car, I said with all deference, "Be back as quick as I can make it, pal."

The young man huddling on the rear seat didn't answer. He was that same Victor Dixon whom I had met earlier this evening. He was still dead. I had brought him along for more than the ride, but so far as he was concerned there would be a slight delay.

I went quietly through the rear gate of the Parke estate—the one used by the milkman, the garbage collector and Cyn when sneaking back from her nocturnal excursions.

Following the cement driveway, I ran into another jolt. Cyn's convertible was not here. She was still on the prowl somewhere. Having murdered Dixon and left his cadaver conveniently in my lap, she hadn't felt it might behoove her to call it a night and head for home. No, she had, instead, gone off on an additional little side-trip. She was taking a short stopover somewhere in her own private nether regions—the devil only knew where!

With both gall and pity in my heart, I saw the windows of Judge Parke's study still shining with their homey green glare. Easing closer and looking in, I found him still seated in his fine morocco chair, beside his antique student lamp, still absorbed in his reading—and still misbelieving that his daughter was soundly slumbering upstairs.

I faded toward the garage, which put me right back where I had begun the evening's spying. Vic Dixon wasn't being allowed a dead man's decent rest, but he wouldn't mind waiting a little longer for his bed in the beyond.

Perhaps forty minutes later, I began observing the smooth skill with which Cyn secretly completed her night's jaunts. First I heard the velvet purr of her car approaching along the side-street. She switched off the headlamps, then the ignition. Swinging in under momentum, she passed through the rear gate, rolled down the gently sloping driveway and braked to a noiseless stop at exactly the spot where the car had previously sat. Left there now, it would appear to have sat stock still all night.

HER next move ordinarily, of course, would be to slip back into the house as unnoticeably as she had decamped from it. But tonight she tarried a moment longer. She switched on the dashlights and bent into the hidden glow to gaze at something closely.

Leaving the shadow of the garage without making a sound, I went to the side of the car. She didn't hear me. She remained bent over, her disarranged yellow hair glistening beautifully, peering at something lying on the flattened palm of one of her hands.

It was a tiny object no bigger than the head of a match, and it gave off a purple glitter. Just a bit of glass. The cheapest sort of artificial gem. A purple brilliant.

It sent up its gaudy sparkles and Cyn's eyes glittered as brightly over it, sharp with spite.

"Whose is it, Cyn?"

As fast as a tripped trap, Cyn's hand closed into a tight white fist. Her widened eyes snapped into my face. She was lovely —her fox soft around her white throat, her red lips parted in 'breathless surprise, her high cheekbones touched by the glow— lovely and at the same time something to chill the blood. Beautiful, endlessly tempting and inevitably—deadly poison.

"Where did you find it?" I insisted. "What does it mean?"

Rapidly she switched off the dash-lights, slipped from the car and stood close, her delicate oval face lifted. "Vince, I—I've been waiting for you, darling—wondering every minute. What have you done with— him?"

Such a luscious little liar! Conscience-less, and expert too, I must admit. If I hadn't seen her silent arrival only a few moments ago, I might have believed that she had been waiting here for me in sleep-less anxiety. But it was far more likely that during her latest journey to those dark parts unknown, she hadn't given her victim a second's thought.

"I'm still trying to decide just what to do with him, Cyn. I haven't had much experience disposing of human corpses. You'll simply have to trust me to do the best I can. I won't let him be traced to you if I can help it. That's really all you care about, isn't it—getting out from under?"

She murmured, "Vince, darling, please don't doubt me." Her lovely face came closer in the starlight.

I took hold of both her arms and she let me hold her there, her mouth lifted to mine. "For heaven's sake, Cyn, let's have it now! Since I'm making myself an accessory after the fact of murder, I think I rate a little inside information as to how I happened to get that way."

She whispered, "Oh, Vince, don't speak of it as murder! Oh, no, Vince! After all, I had to protect myself from the sneaky little rat. It was self-defense, Vince, and nobody can blame me for that. What else could I have done, darling?"

It was a ridiculous plea, but Cyn gave me no chance to answer as she rushed on in a whisper, "Please, darling, we don't dare talk about it now. If Father should find us here like this, he wouldn't like it a bit. Being so old fashioned, you know, he might even turn against you. Tomor-row, darling. As soon as possible I'll tell you how this whole horrible thing was forced on me. Of course I will, darling— but not tonight."

"Now!" I blurted under my breath. "Now, Cyn! Damn it, you've got to at least tell me!"

Suddenly she pulled me close and kissed me swiftly, her lips moist and hot. Then she pushed herself away and broke into a silent run.

In numb resignation and amazement I saw her slip through the door. I could picture her passing within a few yards of her father without a sound to disturb him, then running silently up the stairs to her room. I was still standing there, damning myself for being fool enough to keep on loving this wild-blooded woman —but still loving her regardless—when the lights in her room went out.

Now she was completely guarded by her unwitting father. Until such time as she might choose, she would remain un-reachable by a too inquisitive fiancé.

I asked myself a grim question: What do you do about it when your bride mur-ders a man, then unquestioningly leaves to you the little task of getting her clear of it? Do you drop around to the office of the Chief of Police and say, "Look, maybe I really shouldn't mention this, but my girl has just committed a first-degree homicide. Oh, yes, quite inten-tional, you know."

You do this, do you, in the full expectation that it will mean a juicy coast-to-coast scandal, including possibly the electric chair for the luscious killer, a broken heart and an early grave for a fine public servant, and incidentally turning your own life into a shambles? Or, on the other hand, would that be just a little too righteous?

I was inclined to think so. Yes. All these heartaches and tragedies should be avoided if it was humanly possible. Avoiding it was, of course, entirely up to me. Cyn had arranged it that way. Nobody else could take a hand in clearing up this mess, including the murder. Even though the lady was two-timing her husband-to-be between fittings for her wedding gown, the job was all mine.

So I went quietly back to my car where the dead man had waited so patiently for me to come and dispose of him.

CHAPTER FOUR

Marry in Red

*S*HE *sobbed and clung to me as if never to let me go from her, and she called me by another man's name.*

"*Lee,*" *she whispered.* "*It will be so lonely away from you, darling. Lee—kiss me.*"

She pulled me closer and her kiss was long and hungry. But the end was not far away now. It came steadily closer as our time grew shorter, minute by minute— as more of her blood came to wet her lovely hungry lips.

"Sorry, Vince, my boy, but Cyn's still in bed this morning," Judge Parke said over the phone.

I answered, smiling wryly into the transmitter, "Please don't disturb her, then, Spencer. She needs lots of rest these days." As, indeed, she really did.

"Just nerves," the judge said. "When I spoke to her through her door a while ago, she said her headache had kept her awake most of the night. Too bad, poor child. But it's just nerves, I'm sure. I'll ask her to call you when she gets up, Vince."

"Thanks, Spencer," I said. Only yesterday I had been as blind to Cyn's real nature as her father was today.

Having instructed my secretary to cancel the morning's appointments, I sat at my desk and read again, for the sixth or seventh time, the blackest headlines and the biggest news story on the front page of the *Press*.

The bullet-riddled body of Vic Dixon, special reporter for the *Press,* had been found by a patrolman just before dawn on a footwalk in Lincoln Park. The police so far had not advanced a theory to account for his death. Three bullets had been removed from his body by the coroner and the police were hopeful that "a search" would turn up the death-gun that had fired them. It was not mentioned in which direction the "search" would be made, but it seemed unlikely to invade the home of Judge Spencer Parke.

As to a theory to account for Dixon's death, the cops had none so far, but his city editor had known him to be working on a promising lead to a big story. Dixon, characteristically clam-mouthed, had not let anyone else in on his forthcoming scoop—although he had cryptically promised his city editor that it would be "hot enough to burn the town's ears off." Chief Boshall, however, assured the public the investigation would bring quick results.

Not a word of this was to be trusted. Actually, Dixon might or might not have spilled Cyn's name to his editor. If so, the crash would very shortly knock us all down flat. If not, we could at least gamble on a little time before the law nailed us. There was only one way I could find out—wait.

As to Dixon's corpse, I felt I had done a fair job of planting it deceptively. Deciding not to conceal it, which would have started a widening hunt into places better left undisturbed, I had simply dropped it in a likely spot. Lincoln Park was surrounded by an average residential district, nicely removed from all points of significance, including Laurel Bay, Sycamore Boulevard—and also the corner of Dock and Warehouse Streets.

I had done my best. The simplicity of the false picture—merely a man shot in a public park by someone who had fled without a trace—should be in itself, I thought, enough to baffle the homicide dicks.

Absorbed in edgy thought between readings of the *Press*, I caught myself clearing my desk, tucking things away in its drawers, as if subconsciously expecting to be yanked away at any minute, never to come back . . .

AT ELEVEN that morning, when I phoned the Parke home again, the judge reported that Cyn was still abed, poor child—feeling too indisposed to keep her date for lunch with me, too ill even to talk to me on the phone.

At twelve o'clock the news bulletin on the radio included nothing new on the Dixon murder case except a fence-straddling announcement from Chief Boshall to the effect that "suspects are being questioned and an arrest is expected soon."

At two, talking again with Judge Parke on the phone, I heard that he had summoned a doctor for his daughter. The diagnosis was not too definite: "nervous strain."

"Just as I thought," the judge reminded me. The doctor had left her some sedative pills, with strict orders that she was to remain in bed until thoroughly rested.

"Drop in, say, tomorrow afternoon,

Vince. A long wait, I'm sure, my boy, but no doubt she'll feel much better then. Yes, tomorrow afternoon. Good night, Vince; good night."

Neat. Just as Cyn had wanted it—a device to keep me at a distance, to parry my demands for an explanation, to get me out of her way.

The hell with this merry murderous runaround!

Leaving my apartment, where I'd been wearing tracks in the rug, I stepped out into a thin mist. As I drove across the city the haze grew thicker in the street lights. It put a damp shudder in me. A fog like this, perfect for concealing nocturnal evils, could be just what the devil had ordered for his favorite daughter.

I left my car in the side-street, out of sight of the Parke house, and again went in by way of the back gate. Cyn's car was inside the garage this time. The rest of the picture tonight was the same; pink lights in the windows of Cyn's bedroom upstairs, a green glow in Judge Parke's study.

Moving on like a skulking thief, I passed the judge's windows and paused at the side entrance of the house—the same one Cyn used for her secret exits and returns.

I gave the knob a soundless twist, sidled in, eased the door shut behind me and drifted across the vestibule. Half a minute later I had reached the top of the richly carpeted stairs, breathing fast in tense relief. I had negotiated it expertly enough, without a creak to distract the judge from his book. Cyn had taught me well her furtive ways.

I paused again at the door of Cyn's bedroom, pressed open a narrow crack and looked in. She was sitting up in bed, the covers up to her chin. She was peering at a newspaper, gripping it intently in both hands. She didn't notice me until I pushed the door wider and stepped in.

She gasped then, staring in defiant consternation as I closed the door behind me.

The lights sparkled in her hair and softly modeled her fine oval face. She had never been lovelier—and never, I suspected, so inwardly seething with deceit. She pushed away the paper she had been poring over, and I saw it was a copy of the *Press,* but not one of today's issues.

Speaking as softly as my edged nerves would allow, I asked, "There's something in the paper that interests you more than last night's murder, is there, my sweet?"

"Oh, Vince," she whispered with a lovely smile, flicking back the yellow tendrils of her hair. "All those items about the luncheons and showers for me, and the bachelor parties for you—I've been saving them to clip for our scrap book, darling."

As if to bestow all her warmest attention on me, she dropped the old *Press* out of sight. I sat on the edge of the bed and one of her hands crept to mine as she went on, smiling softly. "You bad boy, you, Vince!" She laughed in delighted intimacy. "Father doesn't dream you're here with me, does he? Wouldn't he be scandalized!"

GAZING at her, I said, "Frankly, Cyn, I've begun to have a few small doubts about our getting married, if we'll be really happy together. Maybe I'd be lonely. I might get to feeling you should spend a night at home once in a while. And looking at it from your side, being married to me might tend to tie you down too much. As painful as the idea may be, my sweet, hadn't you better reconsider?"

"Why, Vince, dearest, I wouldn't *dream* of breaking our engagement!" she said, wide-eyed. "And you would *never* be such a louse as to break it yourself, I know—certainly not this late in the game, with all arrangements made and everything. Would you, darling?"

No. Damn her, no.

"So of course we'll go right ahead and

be married." She added, with her lips twisted a little, "You see, I'm looking to the future. I'll feel so nicely *secure,* being Mrs. Vincent Reece—the wife of such a clever young lawyer—and especially so after he becomes our shining new district attorney."

She laughed again, softly and mockingly. In an upsurge of resentment, I gripped her arm.

"So to you I'm a convenient sort of double life insurance! It's nice to know. But for your own good, you'd be smart not to hold out on me like this. Let's have it now, Cyn—the real reason you killed Dixon."

"No, no, Vince, darling, please don't call it that. I had to do it in self-defense, really. The nasty little—"

"Stop that, Cyn. Tell me!"

"Let me alone!" She snapped it out in sudden feline fury. "Clear out of here, Vince!"

"No. I'm going to get it out of you somehow. Sooner or later—"

"Not now, Vince! You don't understand. There's no time for explanations now. Don't try to stop me. I'm warning you, Vince, *don't get in my way!*"

Suddenly, her cheeks afire with unruly heat, she flung the coverlet off her bed and swung her legs out. Startled, I discovered she was already half dressed to go out—in smoke-colored stockings, black blouse and gray skirt. She pulled open a closet, snatched a matching jacket off a hanger. I moved up on her.

"Where to now, Cyn? Not back to Laurel Bay to set another murder trap, I hope. To a pleasanter place tonight, perhaps—a place where you can go without Dixon dogging you?"

Hurriedly she stepped into twinkling black, spike-heeled pumps, not answering.

"Listen, Cyn. I can wait, if I have to, to hear you spill it. After all, this isn't quite the best place for me to beat it out of you. But for heaven's sake, don't risk

another move now. I've asked a few discreet questions in the right places. So far as I've been able to find out, the cops are getting nowhere on the Dixon murder. It's headed for the unsolved file. You'll probably be safe enough—*if* you sit tight. Just don't push your luck too far, Cyn!"

Her eyes flashed and she snapped, "I'm not letting anybody play me for a sucker, Vince! As for you, my handsome groom, remember I warned you to keep out of my way."

She was throwing a gray topper across her shoulders. It swirled like a dancer's cape as she swung toward the door. As I had already realized, an attempt to balk her here would mean violent resistance on Cyn's part—a physical struggle that would surely alarm the judge in his study downstairs. I had to keep it quiet. Just too late, as Cyn swung the door open, I saw that one pocket of her coat sagged heavily.

The judge's gun?

I started after her in sharp alarm—then froze to a standstill. From the hallway, the judge's voice spoke.

"Cynthia! Why, I was just about to look in at you, my dear, to see how you're feeling."

Cyn was closing the door behind her. The judge hadn't glimpsed me hiding inside her bedroom. Not so far. With the skill of a talented actress, Cyn concealed the surprise jolt his unexpected appearance in the hall had given her.

"I'm feeling *so* much better now, Father, dearest. I thought I'd take a little walk, just a short one, to get a few breaths of fresh air after being shut up inside so long."

"There's a fog, Cyn. Getting thicker, too. May not be safe for you to go out alone." He had no notion of how ironic he sounded. "I'll come with you."

"No, no, please don't bother!" Cyn said quickly. "I'm not going farther than the corner. Be gone only a minute, really

—and I'll be back before you know it."

She hurried on too rapidly for the judge to follow. I heard her running down the stairs, her high heels clicking across the vestibule. The judge was again moving in the hall. He went into his bedroom, directly across from his daughter's.

He wasn't aware, of course, that he had me boxed. If I attempted to slip out now after Cyn, he would certainly spot me. I turned instead to one of her windows. Her little "stroll" was already well under way. She had slipped into her car and was silently rolling it toward the street.

Bound where?

FORCED to stay hidden behind Cyn's closed door, with Judge Parke in his room across the hall, I picked up the copy of the *Press* which she had slipped out of sight. It was date-lined two weeks ago. To judge from the wrinkles where she had clenched the paper in her two fists, she had been peering at a half-cut portrait—a theatrically glamorized woman with dark come-on eyes shadowed by drooping eyelashes.

The name printed above her picture was Vera Siles. The caption began, "Café entertainer at Hillbilly Club, close friend of the culprit, being questioned by the police as they continue their widening hunt—"

At that instant Judge Parke's step sounded again in the hall, directly outside Cyn's door. I dropped the paper, stiffened. Then he moved toward the stairs—and I went back to breathing.

But it had been a close squeak. Found here, I would be forced to do plenty of explaining about a few things which I damned well could not explain. Not to Cyn's father, my old friend the judge. And not now. My play was to get the hell out of here and back onto Cyn's dark trail as fast and as quietly as possible.

I waited tensely until the judge was settled again in his study. Then I eased Cyn's door open and slipped away. . . .

One skirmish past the Hillbilly Club revealed that Cyn was inside. Her empty convertible was parked on the direct approach to it—squarely and insolently beside a fire-plug.

A garish poster propped in front of the Hillbilly Club featured the alluring face of Vera Siles, the star attraction at this crusty dive on the fringe of the city's night-life belt.

Going in and leaving my hat with the pretty long-stemmed bandit at the check counter, I found nothing unexpected. Blue lights, tobacco smoke thickening the gloom, crowded tables, an orchestra strumming a muted melody. I was just in time to see the climactic attraction of the floor-show. The thin white beam of a spotlight drilling through the cig fumes played on the teasing face of Vera Siles in person—with not a man in the place looking at it.

Displaying her smooth technique as a stripper, Vera had peeled down to a few bejewelled wisps of gossamer—and spun herself with a glittering whirl to disappear behind a velvet curtain. Loud applause expressed the male customers' deep appreciation of her art. She bounced back for a bow with the curtain draped across her torso, kicking up one heel in a prancing step. As she vanished again she left a spark of danger shining before my eyes. She was wearing silver sandals having high heels encrusted with flashing purple brilliants.

Purple brilliants like the one I had seen sparkling on Cyn's palm last night.

Now a few amber lights cut the murk a little, and with their help I found Cyn. She was perching on a stool at the bar, alone. The show ended, she took her scotch at a swallow and turned away quickly, her face an expression of distilled malice. The natural fragility of it was swept away by a fire of hatred. It was a raging, propelling force inside her as she hurried toward the street.

She saw me and stopped with her eyes narrowed. The thin tightness of her lips was a renewed warning. "Don't try to interfere with me now!" She brushed past me, hurrying. Taking no time to ransom my hat, I got back outside the swinging doors to see Cyn disappearing into the thickening fog down the street.

I caught up with her near her car. Fastening a hand on one of her arms I forced her to pause.

"For the Lord's sake, Cyn, come back home with me!"

"Let me go!" She was breathing fast, and her blue-green eyes, always so lovely before, were smouldering blue-green spite. "*Let me go!*"

"I can't let you, not like this, Cyn! For the judge's sake—for your own—for mine, too. I've got to stop you before you—"

Her lips hissed out a poisonous sound. At the same instant she whipped her right hand up from the pocket of her coat.

Even as the gun swiped at me I couldn't believe she was really doing it. The gun cracked against my temple, then gashed across the bridge of my nose, then struck with malicious power across my mouth . . .

CHAPTER FIVE

Next Stop, Hell

I FELL in a swirling confusion of black pain. When I pushed myself up from the dew-wet pavement, I heard Cyn's high heels ticking rapidly along the sidewalk. Getting to my knees, I heard her pausing—pausing, I could dizzily imagine, to peer back at the lights of the Hillbilly Club.

Like Cyn, I had heard the doorman's whistle flutter its shrill note. He was signaling a cab forward. A lady had just come out of the club alone—and the lady was Vera Siles. She was well covered now in a chic evening wrap—one more valuable, perhaps, than even Cyn owned. A high-class babe indeed. Even the purple glitter of her heels seemed not too gaudy now.

She stepped lightly into the cab, and it veered off cautiously in the fog. At the same time Cyn's car door slammed. Its lights appeared and the next moment she tooled past me, trailing the elegant Vera's taxi.

Still dizzy from the blow of Cyn's gun, I stumbled back to my own car.

It was a double chase in slow motion— a groping through a blind nightmare. Once past the Hillbilly Club, I angled to the right, seeing a red gleam in the haze that could be Cyn's car. It was, I saw when I pulled closer. She must have seen that I was following her again, but she let me come and pressed her own car doggedly after Vera's cab.

A few blocks later, the cab shuttled past me in the opposite direction, empty. It had dropped its tasty passenger somewhere in the region ahead. And this, I saw as a corner sign-post blurred by, was the neighborhood of Dock and Warehouse Streets.

The taxi disappeared behind me, and suddenly Cyn's car was also gone. She had darted into a narrow side-street. When I reached it, not a sparkle of Cyn's lights was visible anywhere. She had parked— was trying to dodge me.

I caught a glimpse of a furtive movement in the fog overlying the sidewalk— Cyn hurrying on afoot. I quickly curbed my car, slipped out and strode after her.

I almost missed her in the thick, smoky murk. She had backed into a doorway in the hope that I would skirt past without noticing her. There was only the faintest glow from the street light on the corner to reveal her ghost-gray presence; but as I turned to her I saw the glitter of the automatic in her fist.

"It's love you're supposed to offer your husband-to-be, my sweet," I reminded her, mumbling with my swollen lips. "Not gun-fire."

She said in a terse whisper, "I meant it when I warned you, Vince. Don't try to stop me!"

I nodded slowly. "I can see that I'd better stop trying. The best I can do is cover up for you somehow."

Her eyes brightened with an evil sort of triumph. "Why, how understanding of you, darling—but then, you're always such a sweet lad." Then her lovely lips grew malevolently thin again. "Go on back, then, Vince, darling. I'll handle the rest of this alone—and handle it very well, too."

I gazed at her in silence. Then I shrugged and turned away. Cyn was too possessed with vengeful impatience to wait to take her next step. I hadn't gone four paces when I sensed that she had disappeared from the doorway.

I turned back quickly. The door was now standing ajar. She had opened it and slipped in. The gleam shining inside came from a pencil flashlight in Cyn's hand.

She was quietly climbing a long, steep, enclosed flight of stairs—going up with the stealthy, silent tread of a cat.

I recognized this building. I had come here once, not long ago, with Judge Parke. It was part of an estate of which he had been appointed the executor. During the war it had housed a plastics concern, but now it was vacant. It was no puzzle how Cyn had come by the key. She had simply stolen it from her father's desk.

She paused on the stairs, her light aimed down. Her long slender fingers picked up a tiny pellet that sparkled purple. Another brilliant dropped from the heels of Vera Siles' silver sandals. No doubt Cyn had found the first one on this same flight of stairs.

Now she continued climbing the stairs with the tense grace and silence of a cat about to pounce with claws bared. Still absorbed in her purposes, she didn't notice me sidling in from the street. As I went on after her, climbing as noiselessly, I saw a closed door at the top of the stairs. Be-hind that door was something that had possesed and dominated Cyn's whole beautiful being to the point of murder.

She paused at the door. With consummate care she turned the knob. Opening it a crack, she bent to peer in. Her whole body grew tense. Suddenly she straightened, pushed the door wide open with a banging slam. She stood there in candlelight with the automatic leveled in her hand.

From the room beyond came Vera Siles' short, stifled scream of fright. I couldn't see beyond the platform at the top of the stairs above me. Cyn stood there on her fine legs, silhouetted in the candlelight, aiming the gun in.

"You're really an ungrateful rat, aren't you, Lee?" she said.

Her answer was silence in the room beyond. She moved forward through the door. I went up quickly. Cyn may have heard me, but she didn't turn a single glance over her shoulder. She was too hotly intent on keeping her gun aimed at the two targets standing there in the candlelight.

THE candles burned on a wooden crate, their shine too dim in the vast room to show through the paint-film on the second floor windows. The flickering flames were reflected in the white face of Vera Siles and the dark, feverish eyes of the man.

I recognized him. I had been the one, after all, who had introduced Cynthia Parke to him at one of his lavish cocktail parties months ago. His name was Shannon. I could see now, with grim clarity, that more had happened during those ensuing months, between Cynthia and Shannon, than I had had any reason to suspect.

Shannon looked haggard now, but before becoming a fugitive from a murder rap he had been a very suave, and well-heeled lad, running his three illegal but lushly prosperous gambling rooms. He had had quite a connoisseur's taste in women also. His bad break had come when an argument had worked up to a fatal shooting. The other man, unfortunately for Shannon, had happened to be a detective sergeant on the vice squad. Since the police did not feel too kindly toward a cop-killer, Shannon had been forced to abandon his plush casinos and all his classy babes and take it on the lam.

Correction: all his classy babes except the classiest one named Cynthia Parke. She had been keeping him safe for herself. The police were slightly mistaken in believing they might capture him in Toledo at any moment; he had been right here in town all the time, snugly hidden under Cyn's pretty wing.

It was clear now that this was what Vic Dixon had suspected. In the hope of finding Shannon, he had been watching Cyn; and Cyn, aware that someone was tailing her, had been forced to stay away from Shannon. She had had to get rid of the tenacious Dixon before she dared return to Shannon's hiding-place.

She saw now, bitterly, that hiding him had not given her the exclusive rights to his embraces.

"Quite an ungrateful rat, aren't you, my precious?" she said, her voice loaded with venom. "All this while I've kept you safe from the cops—and this is how you thank me. You let me risk my neck for you—while you two-time me with this cheap, two-bit stripper."

Vera was tight with fear, staring hypnotically as Cyn moved closer to Shannon.

Shannon said in his low, suave voice, "Come on, now sugar, easy with that gun. Why, Vera, here, is an old pal, that's all—like a sister to me, honey. I'll tell you all about it if you'll just sort of ease up with that gun."

"Of course, darling," she purred at him Then, like the crack of a whip, "After I've blown you both into the middle of hell with it!"

Shannon had no chance to escape the gun-blast. He tried; his right hand sprang inside his coat, to the shoulder-holster strapped there, but he couldn't complete the grab before Cyn's first shot struck.

The bullet gashed his right bicep and flung his whole arm back, limp with shock. His numbed fingers dragged his revolver out loosely. It dropped to the floor, and the scramble that followed was frantic and deadly.

Both Vera and Cyn cried out shrilly and sprang to snatch up the revolver. Cyn's automatic slammed out another bullet that caught Shannon in the back as he turned. A metallic rattle far outside the candle-light, mixed with the rocking reports, told that this second slug had pierced the soft middle of Shannon's body. He stumbled, sagged to one knee and tried vainly to rise as Cyn sprang past him. She grabbed up the revolver before Vera's hand reached it and turned it swiftly on her.

The first bullet from the revolver struck Vera through the neck. She fell back stiffly as Cyn blasted her with the second full in the face. He face was a splash of blood and splintered bone as she fell, loosely, without a whimper.

Then Cyn stood still, facing Shannon, obsessed with a fiendish fire of revenge. He was still bent on one knee, still striving to get to his feet. She stood there with her eyes blue-green fire, her fine sharp teeth gleaming white in the candle-shine, his own gun in her white hand pointing with inexorable finality.

She shot him once low in the stomach. Then, as he toppled forward and flattened out on the floor, she shot him again in the back. Three times. When she stopped blasting bullets into him it was because the dead man's gun was finally empty.

It had taken only a few chaotic seconds. Cold with horror, I was stumbling toward Cyn. I had no weapon at all. She dropped the emptied revolver as she whirled away and slashed at me with the automatic. It flashed past my upthrown arm and slammed against the side of my head. I staggered as Cyn ran past me, back toward the stairs. Then I heard her shriek.

When I turned she had vanished. Another scream mingled with loud thumping noises on the steep stairs. They ended far below. Then the whole place was tomb-like.

I took up a candle and went down the stairs. In her furious haste Cyn had tripped—caught one of her spike heels at the very top of them. She had plunged down the while steep flight. She lay now just inside the street door, moaning a little, unable to move. After a few minutes' examination I saw clearly enough how badly she was hurt—how desperately fast she must have help at the nearest hospital.

She had stuck her neck out for Lee Shannon; and now her lovely neck was broken. . . .

HER heart-beat was wild. I felt the swift surging of it as she lay there with her blue-green eyes gazing up, wide and soft with yielding—the ultimate yielding of death.

"Darling," I whispered. "Darling. . . ."

She didn't speak. Her red lips were parted and trembling on silence. Just her fast breath came from them, her little jerky pulled-in sobs.

"Darling," I whispered. "This is it. Not the way we expected—but this is it. . . ."

This was the pay-off. She was in desperate need of a doctor, yet I couldn't let her be found here. Not here where her second and third victims lay upstairs, shot dead in her jealous fury. Moving her would be risky, yet somehow I had to get her to a hospital, and fast.

From the hospital, of course, the news that Cynthia Parke had been brought in, critically injured under strange circumstances, would go straight out to the *Press* and the police.

This was it.

First I stuffed the judge's automatic into my pocket. Then I lifted Cyn in my arms, very gently supporting her head. Her eyes pleaded with me to help her and her breath broke in wordless sobs. The nerves pinched by the shattered bones in her neck were short-circuited and her heart-beat was wildly swift as I carried her through the door, out into the secret world where the fog would cloak and guard us.

The blood on her lips was only a fleck then—but soon another drop crept out, making a thin scarlet line wavering and reaching slowly toward a dark bruise on her chin.

I held her close and said, "We can't get away from it now. This is a one-time thing. We can never escape it—at least never in this world. We've got to pay the piper for this merry little dance of death, baby—both of us."

I carried her along that bleak street, through the fog, back to her car, while her breath broke fast and her heart-beat stayed wild. She knew as certainly as I did that there could be only one ending now.

As gently as possible I lifted her into the car and put her on the seat. There, with a vibrant impulse, she stirred. Her hand closed hot and tight on mine and she whispered, "Lee . . . Lee!"

Her mind was enveloped in an evil dream. I was no longer there to her fading senses. She had even stopped knowing that she had killed him. She was back again in the arms of the only man she had ever loved. She sobbed and clung to me.

"My darling Lee. . . . It will be so lonely away from you, darling. Lee—kiss me."

She pulled me closer and her kiss was long and hungry. She sighed in sweet contentedness—so tender now.

Then her breath quickened again. Her eyes stared at blackness and her pulse became an even wilder beat. More of her blood came to wet her lovely lips. And then, after a last paroxysm, she died.

For a long time I sat there, gazing deep into the fog. Cyn would not need a doctor now. I would not need to rush her to a hospital. But the rest was still there—the blood she had spilled, the reporter waiting for his grave, the two corpses cooling in the loft, and lovely Cynthia Parke dead of a broken neck.

I slid under the steering-wheel, started the motor, switched on the headlamps. I drove carefully, turning back to Sycamore Drive. One block from the Parke home I stopped the car. For a few tight minutes I sat there listening through the murk. Then in the respectable quiet I slid off the seat and gently pulled Cyn's lifeless body into my arms.

I half ran along the fog-drenched street, her dead weight a dragging burden, until I came to a panting stop at the excavation in the street just past the judge's home.

"This won't hurt you, darling," I prom-ised her softly, holding her carefully.

I shoved her against the light wooden barricade. It moved with her as I pushed. Suddenly it dropped over the brink; and as it fell, splintering, I flung Cyn's body into the dark, deep hollow.

I heard it strike with a thump. Dirt spilled lower with it. It rolled loosely into the pipe-laced depths of the cavity, beyond the reach of the gleams of the lanterns.

"Good-by, my pretty bride," I whispered. "It's a poor grave, I know. . . ."

I stiffened then, hearing footfalls. Someone was hurrying forward along the sidewalk. The flicker of a ready flashlight warned me it might be a cop. Fading rapidly back in the mist, my presence hidden, I saw him stop where the guard-rail gaped and turn the beam of his light into the hole. . . .

*　　*　　*

I sat quietly, with my head bowed.

Judge Parke sat straight and still in his fine morocco chair in his study, his face deep-lined, a trace of tears in his eyes.

"I know," he said softly. "Yes, I know Cyn had just gone out for a little walk. She would be right back, she said. She must have wandered too close to the curb and missed her step—perhaps because she was so absorbed in thinking about plans for her wedding."

"Yes, sir," the cop said respectfully. "She—she didn't fall far, you know, sir. Sometimes a little fall like that is—enough. I mean—it's just as if she's asleep, sir. She's still as pretty as I used to see her, drivin' by with a sweet smile for me. I— I'll miss her too, sir."

The judge sat silent after the cop backed out. He would feel very lonely later tonight, with his daughter gone; but the worst of the ordeal was right now. A reporter from the *Press* was cooling his heels in the vestibule, and soon the telephone would begin ringing as the shocking news spread—friends endlessly voicing their futile condolences. For me, the bereaved groom, there would be a bit to go through, too—some of it involving a few details which no one else would ever know.

I was mulling them over when the judge rose. "Vince. . . . In the midst of life there is death, my boy. We feel it most keenly at a time like this, when happy plans must be abandoned. How odd it is, Vince—how odd and how bitter it is that now, instead of a wedding, we must arrange a funeral. It must be a small one, Vince, and very quiet."

I was thinking that somehow I must manage to spirit Cyn's car back tonight without the judge's knowledge. As for his automatic, I hoped to find a chance soon to clean it and slip it back into his desk, along with the key Cyn had stolen. I would also phone headquarters an anonymous tip as to where Lee Shannon could be found. Both Shannon and the Siles woman had been killed with the revolver belonging to him, which would be found alongside their bodies. As for the punishment my face had taken, I could simply answer that I had tripped and fallen downstairs.

All threads between Shannon and Cyn were cut, so far as I could see. Dead, Cyn was actually safer than she had ever been alive. . . .

"I was saying, Vince, that the funeral must be a small, quiet one."

"Yes, a simple funeral," I agreed quickly. "Every detail in the most impeccable taste, as befits a woman of Cyn's fine quality."

THE END

THE CARELESS HANGMAN

Back around the turn of the century, John Gales of Chicago made a murderer's peace with his Maker and got ready to mount the gallows. He had been tried and convicted; all appeals had been made and found wanting. When they came to get him in the morning, he had nothing to say and so said nothing.

He still asked no questions when, instead of the gallows, guards took him to Joliet, put him in a cell and left. For a quarter of a century he maintained a discreet silence—then he wrote the governor and asked how come. And how about a pardon?

Authorities looked into the thing and found somebody had made a mistake—how, who, or what kind, was not clear. But they pardoned John Gales.

Carboldt guided yacht-borne Brade and his restless bride to the gem-laden cave of Shan—where waited the . . .

Sepulchre of the Living

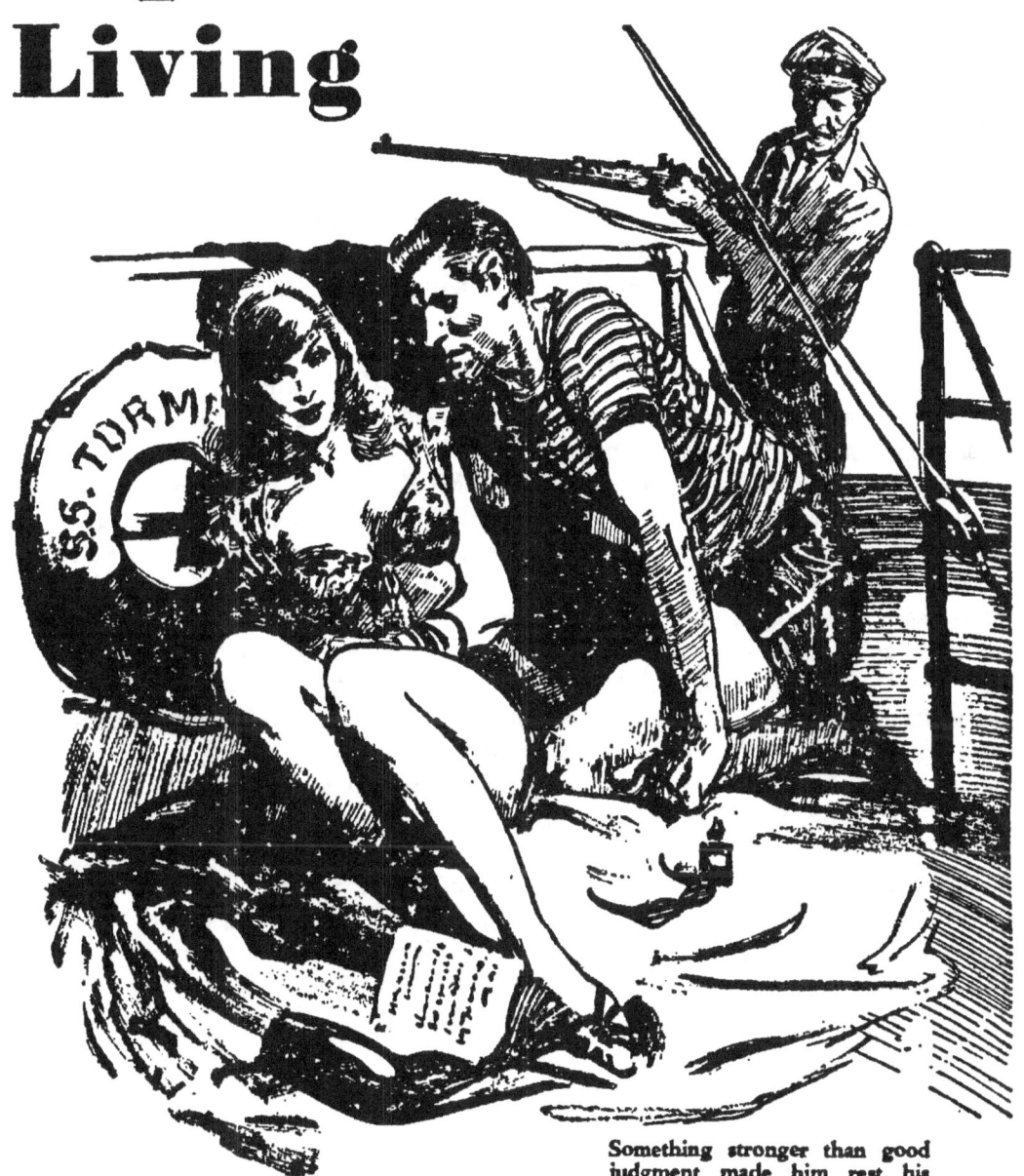

Something stronger than good judgment made him rest his hand against her back. . . .

By Scott O'Hara

HIGH up, high against the roof of the world, on the shoulder of one of the tall mountains of Ceylon, there is a cave mouth. From the cave mouth can be seen the blue stretched silk of the sea, the jeweled green of the jungle, and the misty line where they merge. It is an ancient cave, and in that cave lived the last of the Veddas, chased into mountain hiding by the sons of Singha.

The man who sits in the cave mouth has the tired, brittle face of a scholar, but the thin gray beard clouds the clean lines of cheek and jaw. He hasn't a scholar's eyes, but rather the mild, trusting eyes of a child. The frayed edge of white trousers half conceals the festered bites of insects, and the gray hair is tight curled on his lean chest. His hair is long, and, as he looks down the shattered slope of the hill, he plays with bits of blue glass which catch the sun.

The simple hill people feed him, and he is fast becoming a legend among them. A legend to be treasured, not to be reported to the harsh young British resident who is new in the area.

When he sees the movement in the brush, sees their tight, tan bodies, the bright sarongs as they come out of the edge of the jungle bringing him his food and water, he reaches quickly to one side, slips a flat stone from the side of the cave mouth and shoves the bits of blue glass in against the damp earth before replacing the stone.

The Singhalese come to him with solemn faces. They are feeding a legend, feeding a child of Buddha.

* * *

Dr. James K. Carboldt looked down at his lean legs, inspecting the degree of redness. The yacht, *Torment,* hissed through the greased blue swell of the South Pacific with a muttering hum of diesel power.

He was stretched out on a bright canvas deck chair, lulled by the gentle rise and fall of the trim white yacht. In his own shadow a tall, cool drink rested on the deck beside the chair, and the ice clinked musically with the gentle roll of the ship.

He decided that his legs could stand a bit more tanning. He looked down at Laura, Mrs. Leslie Brade, stretched out face down on a blanket on the deck, appreciating the warm, golden lines of her back, yet feeling oddly uncomfortable in looking at her.

She was creating a difficult situation between him and Leslie Brade, the owner of *Torment.* James Carboldt had spent a great deal of time lately wondering if she was conscious of the way her manner was building up the strain between Leslie and himself.

Laura Brade was a thinnish girl with dull blonde hair which she wore stretched back so tightly that it seemed to narrow her eyes. She wore harlequin glasses which always seemed to have slipped a bit down her short nose. She was tense and quick. A Wellesley graduate, she called herself a 'parlor intellectual' and made quiet fun of the fact that in marrying Leslie Brade she had tied herself up to fifteen million dollars.

Leslie Brade was sitting out on the fantail wearing brief, flowered trunks. Beside him was a pile of empty tins, a box of ammunition. He sat up straight, his strong feet planted against the deck, the slim, deadly target rifle aimed out over the stern. The broad leather sling cut into his arm. The end of the barrel moved as he traced the can in the dancing wake.

When the rifle spat, it was a thin, whip-lash sound. James Carboldt watched the quick play of small muscles across Brade's shoulders, and felt that there was something almost coarse about such brutal strength. Brade had crisp black hair that was thick on his body, sprouting even from the tops of his shoulders, unfaded by the sun that had turned his skin a mahogany brown.

Leslie Brade turned around with a grin and said, "Hey, you sleepers! I've knocked off the last four without a miss."

"Give him a merit badge," Laura said sleepily. She lifted her head and looked at James. "Say, son, you're on the pinkish side."

"I'm too lazy to move," Carboldt said. "Where does that thick-headed husband of yours get his energy?" He reached down, fumbled for the glass, lifted it and finished the drink.

Laura looked at him with the odd intentness that was new with her, and sat up. She took the suntan lotion, handed it up to him and said, in a small girl voice, "Do my back, huh?"

Carboldt grunted as he sat up. She turned her golden back to him as he unscrewed the top and poured some of the pale lotion into the palm of his hand. He was conscious of Leslie Brade's glance on him. To cover his own slight confusion, Carboldt said, "Why don't you grease this luscious form? She's your wife."

"You're handier," Brade said, and there was a small edge in his voice. James glanced at him. Brade had a wide smile on his blunt, swarthy, good-natured face, but the eyes weren't smiling.

Carboldt spread the lotion quickly, highly conscious of the smoothness of the skin under his fingers, the taut, well-knit feel of her. The rifle cracked again and he knew that Brade was once more looking out at the tin dancing on the waves.

Something stronger than good judgment made him rest his hand against her back, holding it very still. He felt her press back against his hand and he took it away quickly. He capped the lotion, set it on the deck and leaned back in his chair.

Laura said, "Thank you," in the same small voice. Her face was turned toward him, her eyes almost shut against the sun. He watched her face, saw the tip of her small pink tongue slowly moisten the upper lip. The rifle cracked again, and this time it made him jump, though he had heard it most of the afternoon.

After a time James got up and padded down to his cabin. He took a quick shower, changed to light linen trousers and a white mesh shirt. He sat on the edge of his bunk and lit a cigarette, telling himself that he was going to have to be very careful. This last little tableau had been more direct than anything that had gone before. Much more direct.

He wondered about Leslie Brade. Something about the thoughts of Brade's thick, muscular body intermingled with the memory of the smoothness of Laura's back sickened him. He wondered how much he thought of Leslie Brade.

Once there had been no question. As a geologist, Dr. James K. Carboldt had served in S.E.A.C. with OSS, as a civilian. Leslie Brade had been Captain Brade, and outside of the fact that it had been rumored around the headquarters that Brade had a great deal of money, Carboldt knew nothing about him.

Then, suddenly, they were partners in a mission—air-dropped in the Shan Hills along with three Burmese, ordered to contact an armed group of Kachin irregulars. The radio had been lost in the airdrop, along with the medicines. The drop had been observed by Japanese agents.

The mission was a failure. There was only one way out, to travel north, to avoid Jap patrols, to join the Stilwell forces in the Hokaung Valley. In the second night they had become separated from the Burmese. On the fifth afternoon Brade took a sniper slug through his shoulder and between the two of them they had held off a small Jap patrol until dark. Then, half carrying Brade, Carboldt had gotten the two of them away.

Brade was out of his head for days, and then he began to mend. He mended just in time to take care of Carboldt who collapsed with fever. After an untold period of agony, they had been picked up by a patrol of the Chinese 28th Division.

Their beds had been side by side in the Calcutta General Hospital. They were invalided to a rest camp in Ceylon, near Galle. When they were strong they swam and did surf riding.

Dr. James Carboldt found that though he was only two years older than Leslie Brade's thirty-one, Brade had an outlook on the world that made him, in many ways, a child. Protected by wealth from the cradle on up, he had no realization of what it had cost Dr. James K. Carboldt to become a young geologist with a growing reputation.

But despite the differences in background, in outlook, in intellectual integrity, they got along very well. Each knew that his life was owed to the other.

Near the end of their sick leave, they went to a small hotel in Ratnapura, and one week they followed a small stream up into the mountains. It was just after the monsoon season, and the stream bed was full of school children searching for topaz, sapphire, other semi-precious stones washed out of the hills by the monsoon rains. They went high into the hills, and Carboldt looked at the rock formations with the eye of a geologist.

He found a narrow cut through a rock slope and he said to Brade, "Les, I'd bet everything you've got that right down in there you'd find more stuff than they dig out of those mines down near Ratnapura in a year. All the conditions are right."

James Carboldt thought no more about it. After he went back to the states and severed his connection with OSS, he took a job with a small oil company in the Southwest for a time. After that, since he had certain findings that he wanted to publish, he took a position teaching in a university in New York City.

Two weeks after his findings had been published and three days before the school term was over, he ran into Leslie Brade on the street. They went into a cocktail bar and talked about the war and the future. He found out that Les Brade had been married for six months to a girl named Laura Nettleton, and that Brade was as childlike as ever about what he wanted to do with his life. He told Brade that he was temporarily at loose ends himself.

TWO weeks later James Carboldt took his bags aboard the *Torment*. The agreement was that they would go back to Ceylon to find that cut in the hills. They would share alike in anything that Carboldt was able to find in the way of gems.

There was a crew of eight aboard the *Torment,* and just the three passengers. Laura looked on the whole project with mild amusement.

During the long trip down the eastern seaboard, through the canal, out across the Pacific, the trip had been a form of perfection. Both Laura and James reveled in it, but to Leslie Brade it was an experience often repeated, too familiar to be remarked on.

They stopped at every port that offered amusement and the three of them were always together.

The present tension had started five days ago. Laura had started it without seeming to do so. She had done it by treating Brade's ideas with derision, Carboldt's ideas with respect. She had done it by constantly watching Carboldt with an intensity that was embarrassing.

She handled herself in a way that was completely casual, and yet, merely by her very casualness, she seemed to highlight the intensity of her feeling for Carboldt. Her every action, every word, was a stinging criticism of Brade, revealing the contempt that had grown out of the realization that to a mature individual Brade was a wealthy child—a bore—a creature fashioned cunningly of muscles and money.

James Carboldt finished the cigarette and flipped it out the open port. His future course of action was clear. He would have to avoid Laura during the remainder of the trip to Ceylon. He would work at his trade in Ceylon and see what could be recovered from the deep cut in the rocks. Then, making some sort of an excuse, he would leave the two of them and fly home.

He went back up on deck and joined Brade on the fantail, borrowed the rifle and missed a particularly large tin with six shots until it was far out of range.

Brade laughed. "Jim, you've got no coordination. You're the brain and I'm the brawn. Let me show you."

He flipped a tin back into the wake, waited until it was a hundred feet off the stern and then fired three shots in rapid succession. Carboldt heard the distant click as the lead hit the tin, watched the tin fill up and sink.

Brade laughed again. An albatross which had been circling the yacht sped low over the water, the thin graceful wings motionless, made a wide turn and began to drift back up wind toward the stern.

Brade said, "Scare him," and fired a quick shot.

The big bird folded its wings and dropped into the waves. It disappeared astern, looking like a piece of white cloth thrown carelessly into the water. Laura stood behind them, her tanned legs braced against the roll.

"That was a foul thing to do!" she said flatly.

Brade smiled uncertainly. "I didn't think I'd hit it, Laura."

"Thinking is an art you'd better leave to others, Leslie."

His smile was still tight against his lips. He looked as though he had run a long distance. "Like Carboldt, maybe."

"Maybe," she said quietly.

He dropped the rifle on the deck, stood up quickly and walked back along the deck. They turned and saw him go down the companionway.

Laura turned and followed Brade. Carboldt sat and looked out across the sea, at the dusk that was touching the eastern horizon. . . .

When the sea had turned from cobalt to gray, he went down to the small dining alcove off the galley and found that only two places were set at the rubbed wood table.

The mess boy said in his soft voice, "Mrs. Brade says for you to eat now, suh."

He had just begun to eat when Laura came and sat opposite him. She had bluish streaks under her eyes.

After the mess boy brought her dinner, he raised a questioning eyebrow at her. She said, "Oh, the big baby was mad because he got scolded and he did like he always does. He went down to the cabin and sulked, and while he sulked he drank scotch out of the bottle and finally passed out. I guess he thinks that he punishes me that way. He's in there snoring and he won't wake up until noon tomorrow, when he'll be cross as a bear."

"You've been a little rough on him lately, Laura."

She widened her eyes. "Me? Rough? What on earth do you mean?"

"You talk to him as though he was a little kid and you laugh at his ideas and—Well, it's hard to explain."

She nodded gravely. "I see. And you think I ought to hang on his every word and tell him how astoundingly bright he is?"

"Don't make it hard for me. I shouldn't have said anything in the first place. It's just that I don't think you appreciate him, Laura. He's kind and he's decent and he's good natured and—"

"And he has fifteen million dollars, more or less."

"Is that important?"

"Laddy, it is to me. It is to me. I got well fed up with being a church mouse. You can think what you want, Jim, but if I had enough money, I'd leave him at once. Maybe that makes me a harsh word. I don't care."

He looked down at his plate. "I guess

maybe I can understand. I never thought about having a great deal of money. I've been contented to work and do a good job. But this trip has been odd. I look at this yacht and the money it represents, and I wonder why I haven't got all this instead of Les. With his money, I'd visit every part of the world that has any interest from a geological point of view. I'd equip expeditions. What does he do with it? Nothing but enjoy himself."

She grinned crookedly. "There's something in that, too, Doc."

"Well, we're hexed now, anyway. That albatross'll get us sooner or later. But, just for the sake of peace and friendship, Laura, make out like you hate me for the rest of the trip."

"You flatter yourself, Doc. I think I do hate you," she said quietly.

He was astonished. "Huh?"

"Yes, I hate you because you are someone to talk to. Someone who can talk sense. I hate you because I'm a girl married to a muscular hulk with all the fine intellectual developments of an amoeba. I even hate you because you don't have any money."

After dinner they went on deck and stood side by side at the rail while the soft Pacific night breeze touched their faces.

He told her of the mission that he and Brade had gone on, and he worked into the story all of the good points about Leslie Brade that he could think of. It was a eulogy of Brade, and she made no comment.

At last he stopped, and she turned quickly against him, her arms around his neck, her quick lips on his own. After a moment she tilted her head back, looked up into his face and said, in a thick whisper, "Tell me some more pretty things about Les, darling."

THE yacht was left in Colombo harbor, clean and shining among the gray and red lead of the battered freighters. They reported in at the American Consul's office near the harbor, stated their intention of staying up in the hills for a month or so, but avoided letting him know the real reason.

They bought supplies at Colombo, and rented a car with Singhalese driver to take them up to the Rest House at Ratnapura. They sat on the upper porch of the Rest House and looked off across the towering hills while they drank arrak and honey liqueur, and Leslie kidded Laura about the hardships of the walk up the stream bed and told her that she probably would have to be carried.

Laura had been very good during the latter part of the trip. James guessed that she had sensed the latent danger in Brade, and she had softened her derision of him to something that seemed as flattering as kind words. Brade had blossomed under the treatment. It was only with sudden looks that were like a hint of flame that Laura told Carboldt that, on the inside, nothing had changed. Nothing at all.

Secrecy had made the trip up the stream bed into an adventure. Before they left the Rest House with their heavy packs, Brade had spent an hour with the manager showing him, on detailed government maps, the route which he claimed they would follow. Of course, after they were out of sight of the Rest House, they circled around until they hit the stream they wanted.

They carried food, jungle hammocks, mosquito netting, medicines and tablets to make the stream water drinkable. The going was steep and rocky, and it took them two and a half days to cover nineteen miles to the cut.

In the brush at the edge of the cut, they made a permanent camp. Laura took over the cooking while Brade and Carboldt worked among the rocks of the cut, using the small hand drills to make holes for the plastic explosive that they had smuggled in.

It was difficult and exhausting work, and the billions of insects made it less pleasant than it had been the last time they saw the deep cut across the face of the mountain. The weight melted off Carboldt. Even Brade looked thinner, harder. There were new lines of tiredness bracketing Laura's mouth, and she was inclined to be sharp with both Brade and James.

They found nothing in two weeks, and Carboldt began to lose his confidence in being able to find the pocket of sapphire which he knew existed in the strata. But he didn't let the others see his lack of confidence.

One day the skies turned gray. Carboldt realized that the chota monsoon was nearly due, and they'd be much more comfortable if they could find better shelter. They took a day off and climbed the face of the mountain looking for caves. He was certain that it was a type of rock formation that lended itself to natural caves.

Laura was the one who found it. As prearranged, she fired a shot with the pistol Leslie had given her, and when they found her she was busily chopping the thick vegetation away from the mouth of a cave with a high, wide entrance.

As soon as they found out that it was dry inside, they went down, packed up and struggled up the rocky slope with the hammocks and bed rolls. The first rain began a half hour after they moved in. Brade set up the little gasoline stove and Laura began cooking the evening meal.

James Carboldt dug in his bag and got the flashlights, gave one to Brade, and the two of them explored the cave which stretched far back into the hill. From time to time Carboldt flashed his light on the vaulted roof to make certain that the rock was firm. After fifty feet the cave widened and turned almost a right-angle corner.

Carboldt walked with the flashlight in his left hand, his right hand sweating on the butt of the revolver. The floor of the

cave was a jumble of rocks and there was something about the silence that was oppressive. He could hear Brade's quick breathing.

"Big enough, isn't it?" Brade said in a low tone, his voice sounding hollow.

"Better whisper. Otherwise you might set up vibrations that'll knock some of the ceiling down on us."

Around the corner the cave stopped abruptly. Carboldt shone his light on the wall and then swung it around at almost floor level, looking to see if there was a smaller exit out of the place.

He gasped and Brade's hand fastened tight to his arm. They walked over and looked down at the jumble of dark bones, at rotted bits of leather and cloth. There were two gray skulls. On closer examination, they saw that the skeletons were complete, the jumbled effect resulting from one body having fallen half across the other. The bone of one skull was badly fractured.

Beyond the two skeletons was a small wooden box, about three feet long, two feet wide and a foot high. Corroded metal handles were set into the ends. The box looked firm and solid.

Brade grunted and stepped over the bones, fumbled at what looked like a wide copper hasp. James Carboldt stepped to one side so he could see. Brade got his fingertips under the edge of the lid and strained, the veins standing out on his forehead.

Something cracked and the lid came up slowly. Inside were a number of small leather sacks. Brade grasped one of the sacks and the ancient leather powdered in his hands, the jewels that it had contained spilling out and falling in among the other sacks, winking up at the light with beams of rich amber, green, red and deep blue.

Brade picked up a handful of the stones and stood up suddenly. Carboldt felt weak and dizzy. "What do you figure?" Brade asked.

"I—I don't know. Let me see one." He held it in the flashlight's glare. "I'd say it was an emerald. Probably cut a long time ago. This isn't Ceylonese stuff. Probably the emeralds came from India, those rubies from Burma, the aquamarines from Kashmir. Maybe the yellow and blue sapphires were from Ceylon. It would take a long, long time for the leather to turn to dust like that. Eight hundred years. A thousand."

Brade squatted again and tore open some of the other sacks. The piled gems glittered. He reached over and grasped the metal handle at the end of the case and tried to lift it. The side of the box came off with the handle and the gems spilled out onto the rocky floor.

At last they turned and hurried back to the entrance to the cave. The gray daylight shone in on their faces and Laura looked up and said, "What's the matter with you two? Are there ghosts back in there?"

Brade grinned at her, opened his hand and dropped several of the stones into her lap.

She fingered them with wonder. "Real?"

"I think so," James said.

It was difficult to eat. After the meal was over, Carboldt said, "Well, the problem now is to get them down onto the yacht without fumbling it."

"What do you mean?" Brade asked.

"I've been trying to figure how we can do it. There's so darn many of them. We can shove a lot of them into the canteens, melt wax over them, let it cool and then fill the canteens with water. Then we can use the same idea on the gasoline tank on the stove. Maybe bury a few more in Laura's face cream. But that'll only take care of a tenth of the stones. No, we've got to think of a good way to get them all out."

He saw Brade's frown in the darkness. "Have you gone nuts, Jim? I know how these things work. Hell, if they ever found any of these rocks on us, they'd crucify me. I've got a reputation to take care of. Besides, do you think we could market them in the states? We'd be jumped in a minute.

"No, we've got to tell the authorities and let them take over and see if out of the goodness of their heart, they'll give us a small share. If I know my foreign countries, they'll probably give us one flawed ruby apiece and call it square."

Carboldt was suddenly furious. "That's fine for you, Brade. Just dandy! You've got all the money you can possibly use, so why try to get more? But how about me? The deal was a fifty-fifty split. There must be a million dollars worth of gems there. I won't permit you to give my half away along with your own."

"It's not a question of choice," Brade said sullenly. "I can't take the chance, that's all."

"You're going to take it!" Carboldt said shrilly.

Brade looked at him with a slow grin. "Getting a little money hungry, Jim?"

"You're damn well told I am!"

"Boys! Boys!" Laura said. "Take it easy. We'll talk about it in the morning."

They argued for over two hours, and at last, weary and defeated, Carboldt slung his hammock near the cave mouth, wedging climbing pitons into the cave wall. Laura and Leslie spread their bed rolls far back in the cave.

CARBOLDT was awakened suddenly as he was touched and when he opened his mouth to say something, a small warm hand pressed over his lips. He caught the elusive perfume of Laura and knew that she was standing beside his hammock.

She put her lips close to his ear. "Shh, darling. He's asleep, but I'll have to hurry back. He's being unfair about this. Do you love me, Jim?"

He whispered, "Yes."

"Then it will be fixed. That's all I wanted to know. That's all I wanted to know." Her lips brushed his lightly and she was gone.

He stayed awake for a long time, trying to puzzle out what she had meant. At last he fell asleep.

In the morning, when Brade went down the slope to the creek to wash, the bright sun shone into the cave mouth.

Laura, her face very pale, said, "This has got to be quick, Jim. He'll have to die here. It'll look as though a rock fell from the ceiling of the cave. We report the tragedy to the authorities and at the same time we turn over all the jewels we found. In the excitement about the jewels there will be no suspicion. They'll say that we couldn't have done such a thing unless we were trying to get away with the jewels. Let them have the jewels. I will have his money and then we can be married."

He looked at her white lips with complete disbelief. He stammered, "But I can't—I couldn't—"

"Remember what you said last night, Jim. You'll have nothing to do with it. If I were free, would you marry me?"

He thought of the yacht, of the fine cars and clothes and homes. He tried to form his lips over the word, "Yes."

"Shh!" she said. "He's coming."

After breakfast she took the stones that Leslie had given her before dinner the night before and examined them in the sunlight. Her eyes held a soft calmness, a strange content, that amazed Carboldt.

After breakfast he saw the muscles at the base of her jaw knot. She said, "Les, darling. Please take me back and show me that old box again. I'm afraid to go alone."

"Sure, honey."

They stood up together. She glanced at Carboldt and her eyes looked opaque. He felt powerless to make a move. His lips were numb and his palms hurt where his fingernails dug into them. Sweat poured off his face.

He watched them go side by side into the darkness of the cave, heard Laura say, "Oh! Les, dear, I just dropped one of those stones you gave me. It rolled over that way. Will you look for it like a dear?"

Leslie Brade grumbled something about clumsiness, snapped his light on and dropped onto his knees, pawing among the jumble of rocks. They were just at the edge of the complete blackness, so that Carboldt saw them as pale silhouettes against a velvet curtain. He saw Laura stoop quickly, saw her come up with a rock held tightly in both hands, a lethal slab of broken shale.

As she lifted it, held it poised over Leslie's head, James Carboldt remembered the mission, remembered the bitter hours in the wet stinking jungle where he would have remained and died but for Brade's help.

In sudden cold fear, Carboldt yelled, "Laura! No!"

Brade spun around, saw the rock poised above him. He fell to one side as the rock came down, missing him narrowly. With his clenched left fist he hit Laura full in the face, knocking her down among the rocks. The forgotten flashlight shone up on Brade's motionless figure. His right hand stabbed down toward the gun on his hip.

Carboldt snatched his own gun from his holster and said, "Drop the gun, Les. Drop it!"

In answer, he saw Leslie Brade spin and fire at him, saw the gold-orange splat of flame, felt a sledge-hammer blow against the side of his head as he spun down into darkness. Even as he spun down, he felt and heard the full-throated rumble of the moving earth.

* * *

High up, high against the roof of the world, on the shoulder of one of the tall mountains of Ceylon, there is a cave mouth. From the cave mouth can be seen the blue stretched silk of the sea, the jeweled green of the jungle and the misty line where they merge. It is an ancient cave, and in that cave once lived the last of the Veddas, chased into mountain hiding by the sons of Singha.

The man who sits in the cave mouth has the tired, brittle face of a scholar, but the thin gray beard clouds the clean lines of cheek and jaw. He hasn't a scholar's eyes, but rather the mild trusting eyes of a child. Along the right side of his head, above the ear, is an enormous puckered scar.

His hair is long, and, as he looks down the shattered slope of the hill, he plays with bits of blue glass which catch the sun.

The simple hill people come to feed him and their faces are solemn as they come, for they feel that they are feeding a legend, feeding a pure child of Buddha.

It pains them that he refuses to be taken to a better cave. His cave is no good. It is too shallow. A few feet behind him, as he sits, the fresh broken rock stretches in a sloping pile to the cave roof. Today they will try to move him to a better cave and once again he will refuse, politely but firmly.

The hill people discuss him in whispers. Truly he is a man of great piety. They are prepared to hide him from the other white men who search the hills.

UNDERTAKER'S DELIGHT

By John Bender

I saw his tongue slaver across his razor teeth . . . as he crouched to spring.

*My dreams of golden Claire—
and nightmares of faded Elsa
—caged me in the sawdust pit
with my jungle cats.*

◆　　　◆

IN MY eyes, certainly, must have been a look of adoration. I thought that she was lovely. Lovelier than any woman has a right to be. Her soft, darkly golden hair held the light and became a tawny cap that matched so well the dusky gold of her flawlessly silken skin.

When she moved about the small, dank-smelling tent, in that tantalizingly brief and becoming costume, the fascinating litheness of her perfect body was clearly revealed. She was as supple, as steel-under-velvet-looking, as one of my cats—and perhaps that was really what I saw in her. A cat.

A sleekly, beautiful animal for me to train and bend to my will and whip, like Thor, my fine new Bengal. . . .

"Gregor," she said, her voice a flame touching my name, "my robe, please. That's the good fellow." Beneath the golden eyes, her mouth was soft and curved upward at the edges.

I took the scarlet cape from the chair and carried it over to her, across the tiny tent. My fingers, caressing the silk robe, knew no difference when my hands came to rest on her shoulders, save for the warmth beneath them.

She bent her golden head backward, to touch my cheek. The faint musk of her perfume reached me. My hands found their way around her slender waist.

"Gregor," said the golden Claire. "You must not!" She pulled away from me. "Someone may see us!" Her voice was theatrically coy, liquidly teasing.

"Claire, darling!" My words were husky, uncontrolled. "Must you always run from me?"

She didn't answer. Instead, she cocked that lovely head toward the sounds from outside the tent—the noise of milling people, the afternoon audience leaving the main tents and the sideshows of our traveling circus. I could hear the bray of animals against the shuffling of many feet. Someone kicked a guy rope of the tent that we were in, and the entire structure shook.

Claire frowned. "We are hardly private here, my dear."

I was all too keenly aware of that. I cursed the people, the stumbling small-town clodhoppers coursing by in their noisy fashion, the shouting roustabouts, and all who are engaged in the activities of Madden's Marvels, Inc.—the Show of Shows. I cursed any and all intrusions upon my brief moments with Claire de Leon.

She had seated herself at her small dressing table, and was removing the tapes from her slender wrists.

"Was I not excellent this afternoon, Gregor?" She was gay and quite impersonal, now—the performer seeking adulation.

"You were magnificent, you darling. Queen of the high trapeze—" I smiled, matching her coquetry with an air of lightness—"the angel on high."

She laughed. "You tease me, Gregor."

"I love you," I said, before I could damn the admission in my throat.

For a moment a trace of resistance—like the hackles rising on the back of my cat Thor—stiffened the lines of her young face. A pulse beat within the exquisite column of her throat.

"It is not wise to say such things, Gregor. You must not."

In a stride I had crossed to her and swept her into my embrace. Into the soft hollow of her neck I murmured, "My darling, my darling." But she was maddeningly stiff and resistant.

She pushed me from her. Her eyes and mine looked into each other's. Nothing had changed. There was still the question, the decision to be made.

"Elsa?" she said. "Your wife, Gregor? What of Elsa?"

ELSA, indeed, I thought, as I made my way across the emptying circus grounds. It could not go on this way much longer—I was convinced of that. For weeks now Elsa and I had known that there was no love for us to share.

Since we had joined Madden's circus in the spring, our tolerance of each other had grown more thinly disguised, until it became an association fraught with snarls and battling to match the behavior of our tigers in the arena.

It is silly, perhaps, to those of you who have never walked the sawdust pit, that we were bound by more than the laws of marriage or finance. Why not a divorce and settlement, you think? Each to his own devices and paths to happiness— That is a laugh!

Full well I knew the extent of our ten-year-old bonds. For Elsa was the daughter of the famed Fritz Schabel, animal trainer supreme until a cat got him one day in Austerlitz. And I, Gregor Francon, had toured both England and the Continent with the outstanding Rincon circus, and I knew the value of such a collection of cats as ours. I knew the difficulties of assembling a troupe of cats such as these left us by Fritz Schabel.

Ours was the most highly regarded menagerie in the world—put together after years of the most dangerous and exacting training. Neither Elsa nor myself would have relinquished one of our cats to the other. So, you see, how impossible was divorce.

It was clear to me, on that summer afternoon when I knew in my heart's blood that I must have the golden girl, my lovely Claire, that there was but one recourse. Could I do less than rid myself of this woman I was bound to, this faded and unattractive Elsa who had chained me to herself with her cats?

Already I had discussed it with myself a thousand times over, since the first moment I had looked upon the lovely Claire de Leon. Nights I had lain sleepless thinking, planning. . . . I had even dared to voice my thoughts to Claire, one careless afternoon. And in her velvet eyes had come a fear that stopped my breathing for a moment. Love me as she must, from her I could expect no help whatsoever.

It was left for me alone to find a way to attain our escape and our salvation.

I groaned aloud, walking through the torpid summer day. To make it seem that Elsa's death was natural—truly, that was a problem. Hale and healthy as a horse, she was stronger even than myself.

I calculated accidents, ways and means, and discarded all of them. Unworthy they were, and unsafe for myself and my golden girl.

If only there was something. I went to the cages, desperately at odds with myself, uneasy with my problem. . . .

I spent half an hour with the cats—principally with Thor, who was the most sorely in need of discipline. He was the newest of our retinue, a nasty brute, though quick enough to respect the whip.

Twice I broke his snarling surliness with the leaded butt, forcing him to the star-painted stool, venting my undecisive anger upon his quick-footed savagery. He did not like it much; c'est vrai, he did not like me much. I could tell it, and I did not take the chance of turning my back upon him, you can be sure.

He was a magnificent devil, young and impulsive, and cunning as they come. He was a recent addition to our menagerie—an uncle of Elsa's had sent him to us only the month before—and the main tent cage was still somewhat strange to him. I kept him moving, away from his own vicious thoughts, and whipped him to the exit chute when I was done.

I gave my whip and blank-loaded revolver to one of the standabouts, and went on to my quarters. Elsa was there, her pale gray eyes questioning, her hands busy with the pressing of one of my silk, white uniform shirts.

Young Madden, the owner of the circus, was there in our tent as well. A dull young fellow, he had shown a certain kindliness toward Elsa, and she had responded in her loneliness. I didn't think too highly of him, but he kept her, thankfully, from plaguing me the long day through; and in a sense I was grateful to him for this.

He smiled as I came in upon them. "A new routine, Gregor?" he asked with heavy heartiness.

"Thor does not know the gun as yet," I said. "The whip he will respect, but—"

Madden shuddered. "A brute, that boy." He looked for a long second at Elsa. "I wish you folks hadn't added that fellow."

Elsa smiled. "Thor will be all right."

"Yes," I said. "He can be handled. I will bring him into the cage for tonight's performance."

There was a short silence.

"It's your tiger," Madden said, much too casually.

My wife regarded me carefully. She folded my silk shirt for a while longer, then stopped. "You—you are sure he is ready, Gregor?"

"Of course!" I snapped.

I was aware of their glances, and of the heat of my own anger which had risen suddenly. I felt a strange delight in knowing that I would have Thor under my whip for the evening show. "Thor goes in the cage tonight with the others!"

I tossed my jacket on my cot, and smiled at my wife. "Unless you think, my dear, that I shall be too brutal with the whip?"

Elsa's lips grew even thinner; her eyes avoided mine. "As you wish," she said hollowly. "As you wish."

And Madden, clearing his throat uncomfortably, muttered something about some business he had to attend to.

I listened to his footsteps fade in the dirt outside.

Elsa said, "You are disturbed, Gregor."

Had she seen me go into Claire's tent? Did she suspect?

I said, "You will have my scarlet uniform ready for tonight, Elsa," and I lay on the cot, to get some rest before the evening's performance.

The tall thin woman who was my wife said, "The uniform will be ready for you, Gregor."

I closed my eyes and dreamed of my golden girl.

FOR the evening show, Claire's act was before my own. I watched her from the chute leading to the dressing tents, her golden body limned against the darkness of the tent roof. The comparison to Elsa, who stood at my side, was odious and almost beyond endurance.

My wife said, "She is lovely, isn't she?" and I searched her face for hidden meaning to her words. But there was only the blonde, pale features I had once thought attractive. Nothing else. She looked up at me. "You had better get dressed, Gregor."

She had laid out my clothes, as usual, and I dressed hurriedly. Elsa took my cage gun and whip and carried them as we went down the chute toward the performers' arena.

Madden met us as we emerged into the main tent, and he seemed, I thought, nervous and upset.

He looked from Elsa to myself. "All set?"

I nodded. The music blared and I walked toward the big cage, with Elsa just behind me. The handlers were shooing the cats from their small crates into the arena, and the animals were rubbing themselves against the bigger cage as they entered, softly padding their way into the pattern of their trained positions. All but Thor. That brute was nervously pawing the dirt just in front of the entrance.

Elsa said quickly, "He is upset with all the people."

Madden laughed. "Stage fright, eh, Gregor?"

I took the gun from Elsa. The spotlight found us then, and I took the whip from her trembling hand. On the rising chord of music I went into the cage and slammed the door behind me.

I was not thinking of my performance, nor of the cats. I was thinking of Claire, and Elsa, and of what I could do about Elsa. If only there were something I could arrange. Something to look like an accident. . . . I saw Elsa's pale and drawn face just beyond the cage.

Thor came across the circle of the arena, padding insolently. I turned to him, stamped my booted foot hard against the dirt. He snarled and fell away, mixing with the other beasts.

I went forward, to the center of the ring. Thor was growling softly, his purr a dangerous indication of his mood. I used the gun in my left hand, firing its undamaging charge against his tawny coat. He subsided for the moment.

The music rose in blaring crescendo, a prelude to the waltz strains they would play as I performed. Despite the noise of the band, I heard an ominous click behind me. I cast a hurried glance to the rear. The lock on the cage had been snapped fast by Elsa—in defiance of the safety rule which we had worked out.

I was locked in the cage!

The snarling beasts, led by Thor, took my full attention, then. I raised the whip, snapped it toward the renegade Bengal, and jerked my wrist—and saw the whip snap in two.

The whip had been carefully and cleverly severed so that it would break apart!

A rush of panic filled me, for Thor respected nothing but the whip I no longer held. I saw his tongue slaver across his razor teeth, his beady eyes venomous upon my own as he crouched to spring. Desperately I went back, pressing against the locked door of the cage, and even in that moment of horror I could hear Elsa's shrill laughter.

I heard the snarling roar as Thor, unafraid of my useless gun, leaped through the air. The crowd screamed in a collective shriek of terror that matched my own cry of dread. Even as the weight of the brute brought me to the ground, I had a glimpse of Elsa standing next to young Madden, her eyes flaming with hatred as she looked at me. And he, clutching her hand tightly, regarded her with a look of love and adoration that must have been very similar to the way I had looked at the lovely, golden Claire de Leon.

Till Death
Do Us Join

She walked up the steps, trying
to pass him. . . .

*Sandra was haunted by the chameleon man who
stole a march on Paul—and took them to a
midnight funeral.*

By Theodore
Sturgeon

SANDRA opened the door. It was
Golly. He walked in, kicked the
door closed without looking at it,
taking Sandra's arm as he passed her.

He spun her around to him for a kiss.

She wiped her mouth. "I don't like that, Golly."

"I do." He kissed her again. His clothes were not very clean. Sandra stayed passive in his arms, waiting to be released. He pushed her away abruptly, and turned his back. "Paul's been here," he said.

She shook her head, making a tiny negative sound. Golly picked up a severely expensive handkerchief from the divan and tossed it to her. "Ain't yours."

"It is."

He sat down, lit a cigarette, and then looked at her. "With that P sewed on?" He compressed his lips. "I got no use for a two-timing woman, Sanny. Even less for a dumb one."

Sandra's forehead paled, heightening the red on her cheekbones. "If you don't like it, Golly—"

When Golly laughed his teeth showed right up to the gums. He was wiry and slender, with shoulders a bit too wide for his hips. Sandra was always unnerved by his utter relaxation. With Paul, now, she was continually afraid of using bad grammar.

"What's funny?" she snapped.

"You," Golly said, not laughing any more at all. "You really think you can get rid of me just by telling me off?" He folded his arms. "If I ever catch Paul here I'll kill him. You know that."

It was perfectly true, she thought, watching him, trying to build up some armor against his narrow gaze. "Tell *him* that," she said slowly. "He's your brother, not mine. Incidentally, I'm not married to either of you. Not likely to be, either, as long as this feud goes on."

She walked over to him, stood near, knowing that he would touch her if she came an inch closer, knowing that he wanted her to. Her hair was chestnut, and she wore it long, with a rakish part on the left. Her nose was aquiline and her

mouth a little twisted when she relaxed her features. Her brows made her eyes look closer together than they were, so that in profile her face changed startlingly.

No one ever treated Sandra gently but Paul. Paul was funny, though. You never could tell about Paul.... Golly, now, was predictable. Golly was going to get sore, right away, when she got this off her chest. She spoke freely:

"Golly, I like Paul. Can you understand that? Yes, he was here. He'll be here any time he feels like it, any time I ask him to come. I won't have you telling me who can and who can't come here."

A smile sprang to his lips as if it were something caught from his shrugging shoulders. He rose and came toward her. She stepped back, and he continued across to the door.

"I'm not rushing you, Sanny," he said, "but you might as well get used to the idea of having me around. 'Night." The door closed behind him, then opened again. He leaned in and said very softly, "If you see Paul again, he won't live twenty-four hours. You can tell him that from me."

Sandra drew a breath to speak, put out her hand—but he was gone. She stood for a full minute looking at the door, and then went to the divan's end-table and viciously snubbed out his cigarette.

*   *   *

At a dance Sandra had met Paul. He was clean-cut, charming, and wore well cut, soft-toned clothes and perfect collars. From the very first Sandra sensed some lack in him, but could never determine quite what it was. She stopped wondering about it when she met Golly.

In the two brothers she found what she wanted. If Paul had ever reached for her suddenly, wordlessly, kissed her so that it hurt— Well, it would have been Paul. But he never did. Had Golly been soft-spoken and a little gentler, she could have loved him.

And they hated each other so much that it was dangerous for her to see either, once they both became interested.

They hated each other, and yet it was through Paul, in a way, that she first met Golly. She had a date one night with Paul and the bell rang twenty minutes early. She answered it.

"Paul, you're early. Why—you're not dressed. Or—that is Paul, isn't it?"

"It is not, and don't call me that. I'm Golly." He wore a thick black sweater and she did not think he was wearing a shirt.

"Golly? Oh—Paul's brother. He mentioned you once. Come in. Is Paul—"

"Will you stop talking about that dirty heel?" he snapped.

She was shocked. "Wh-what can I do for you?" she asked faintly.

"Nothin'. Hey, stand over here by the light. Hmmm. You're okay. Like to have me around once in a while?"

"Well, I—After all, Mr. Egan—"

"To you my name's Golly." His hands took out a cigarette and lit it, apparently without his knowledge. "Keep away from that big slob."

"Please!" She was certainly not prudish, but she had never met anyone like this before.

He did not apologize. Paul would have, for less. Paul often did. Sandra didn't like this Golly, this inscrutable, impulsive brother of Paul Egan. She didn't like him, and she didn't tell him to go.

He stayed for forty-five minutes and in that time kissed her twice. He left her suddenly without saying good-by, and she sat staring at his cigarette butts for nearly an hour, with her heart beating too fast, before she realized that Paul had broken their date.

Her annoyance turned to puzzlement, and then to the realization that Paul had stayed away because Golly came. She laughed, a conscious effort which made her feel more calm, and spent the evening ironing and wondering how such a poisonous hatred could develop between the two.

Afterward, Golly dropped in at highly irregular intervals. Always, when he entered, it would be with that flashing search of the room, that sniffing of atmosphere. Twice he had sensed Paul's recent presence, and the second time it happened was the occasion of his ultimatum. "If you see Paul again, he won't live twenty-four hours."

Sandra was frankly worried. Although admittedly dramatic, Golly could be extremely thorough. When he decided to kiss her, she got kissed. If he determined to kill Paul— But they're *brothers,* she thought in sudden panic. *Brothers don't kill each other.*

Do they?

Sandra began breaking dates with Paul. Golly, of course, came more often.

She liked him less each time—and she wanted to see him more. The powerful appeal of his arrogant manner almost offset her distaste for the things he did because of it. She deeply resented the advances he made, and in her heart resented him for avoiding those he could have made. She knew, too, that his casualness was neither restraint nor indifference, but a challenging half-interest. Sandra despised herself because she was affected by it but. . . .

PAUL came, finally. She ran to the door, thinking it was Golly, for Paul never came without phoning first. But it was Paul, standing abashed under the porch light.

"Paul! Oh, you idiot! I told you not to come!"

"I know," he said gently. "I know you did. But Sandra, I had to know why, and you wouldn't say. Can't I come in for just a moment?"

She stood aside, reminded too vividly of the way Golly rang and then pushed past her. "For just a moment, then."

He came in and she took his coat wordlessly, nodding toward the divan. He sat down and began to pack his pipe neatly and nervously. Golly smoked cigarettes and left them burning on the edges of tables.

Sandra sat beside him, knowing a little disdainfully that he would come no closer. She waited for him to say something. The silence grew painful. Twice he licked his lips and opened his mouth, and twice he closed it against the pipestem.

Finally he said, "San, please. Why won't you tell me?"

"Tell you what?"

"Don't make it any harder than it is!" he barked, and she was startled by his tone. "Why won't you see me any more?" When she would not answer, he asked, "Have I done something?"

You haven't done anything, you fool, she thought acidly. She said, "No. It's something you won't talk about. You mentioned Golly once, when I asked you if you had any relatives around here. Since then you have always managed to change the subject."

His eyes widened. "Golly." After a long moment he breathed. "Oh. I see." Then he was quiet for so long that she flared up.

"Well?"

"Sandra," he said with difficulty, "there are things that—that—"

"That can't be discussed." She stood up. "So why bother? Good night, Paul."

He stayed where he was, looking at her with wide suffering eyes. "Sit down, Sandra. I'll tell you as much as I can. I'd like you to understand."

She sat down, waited.

"Golly is—is—he hates me."

"I know." She had a sudden, shocking mental picture of Golly's slitted gaze, his quiet, deadly threat. "Why?"

"I don't know," Paul said, and ran his hand roughly through his carefully combed hair. His eyes closed. "You know how—how many stories there have been about—about a man's not wanting to admit to a girl anything concerning—insanity in the family."

"Paul." Her voice was very gentle.

"Golly is a—a— He's dangerous, Sandra."

"I know that, too."

"If I could only—face him, talk to him, I could make him go away and never come back. But he—he—"

"He keeps away from you." She remembered, suddenly, the night Golly had come when Paul was due, and that Paul had not come at all. "Where does he work? Where does he live?"

"I don't know," said Paul worriedly. "The waterfront, a warehouse—somewhere around. I never know. I—Sandra!"

She turned with him. Their faces were close.

"There's a *good* thing in all this," he said. "You wouldn't see me. You thought that if I came here he would kill me, and you wanted to make it—safe for me. You cared enough to—"

She looked as him, his sensitive brow, his tender mouth. "Don't flatter yourself!" she blazed. "I don't want to be the cause of any silly brawls, that's all. If you want to get killed, walk in front of a truck! But don't get me mixed up in it!"

The beginnings of a smile died on his face. He rose stiffly and went for his coat. At the door he paused, but when she did not speak, he went out, closing the door carefully behind him.

That was a lousy thing to do, she thought, and ran out on the porch. "Paul!"

He was at the gate, opening it. He turned and came back.

"I'm sorry, Paul. I flew off the handle."

"That's all right," he said softly. She knew he was still hurt because he did not offer to take the blame on himself. She drew him inside but did not offer to take his coat.

"Listen, Paul. I'm sick and tired of having you two mess up my life. Tell me what's the matter and let's do something about it, once and for all. This thing can't go on any longer the way it is. What's the trouble between you and Golly, anyway?"

He licked his lips. "It's a—a sort of psychosis, Sandra. You've seen it before, surely, but in milder forms. Most brothers—and sisters, too—feel that they are a little incomplete as long as the other exists. This is only an extreme example of it." He put up a hand, for she was about to speak.

"No, San. Don't catechize me about it. It'll work out. You'll see. If I can once get to him, get to know why he—" He shook his head. "I'll make it all right. I'll get rid of him. Trust me, Sandra—please trust me."

She looked at him, and the lip which had begun to curl relaxed again. He was so very sincere, and, for the moment, so very helpless. But he would be able to do something. And he wanted to; he cared desperately about it. Golly, now, Golly didn't care much at all. Not enough to want to do anything but—but—

"I trust you, Paul. But do something quickly, quickly, darling." She leaned forward and kissed him on the mouth; then, crying, ran upstairs.

Paul called her, but she did not answer, and he went away. From her bedroom window she saw him go down the path with his head bowed. At the gate he paused, turned, removed his hat and waved it high over his head. He always did that. Always.

THREE nights later, when she came home, she found Golly on the porch steps, sprawled back as if he had been poured there and half-congealed.

"Well," she said, stopping before him.

"Hi," he said, his arm moving by itself to give her a vague salute. She walked up the steps, trying to pass him. He plucked her from her feet, landing her ungracefully in his lap.

"Damn you!" she said into his mouth. He moved his head away, looked at her somberly, and kissed her forehead. Then he set her on her feet.

Trembling, she marched up to the door and opened it. She knew it would be no use to slam it in his face, so she left it open. She took one arm out of her coat, paused, rubbed her cheek where his unshaven face had rasped it. Paul was always spotlessly clean, fresh-shaven when he came. Why did these two always remind her of each other so? What kind of half-men were they?

She slung her coat on the end of the divan—an act quite foreign to habit—and turned to look at Golly, who was teetering toe-to-heel in the center of the room, staring at her through those narrowed eyes. They were so like Paul's, and yet had such a different light.

"Golly," she said, "I'd like you a lot better if you tried just a little bit to act like a—a gentleman."

"Maybe I don't want you to like me any better."

"Wh-what?"

"Sure. I don't want dames tagging along after me."

"Don't flatter yourself!" She stopped, confused by her use of the same phrase she had hurled at Paul. "What do you want?"

He raised his eyebrows interrogatively and lit a cigarette.

"What did you come for? What do you want?"

"Hm. Peevish tonight," he grunted. He threw his match on the rug and came toward her. She ducked under his arm and picked up the match. He did not try to stop her.

She felt suddenly afraid—afraid with no sense of excitement, afraid even to run from him, because she knew she could never get away.

"You saw Paul the other night."

She had no denial, could find none, could find no voice for one. Her eyes were round.

He stepped close to her, stooped a little to look into her face with his veined-marble gaze, cupping her chin in his hard hand. When he spoke his voice was soft and very gentle, like Paul's. "Oh, Sandra, Sanny, I *told* you not to see him. I told you! Why did you do it?"

"Golly," she whispered. "Don't look at me like that. I—"

He slapped her across the face twice, with the front and back of his hand. When she raised her arms, he hit her hard in the pit of the stomach. As she began to sag his fist crashed into the side of her jaw. She hurtled backward, struck the divan and slid to the floor.

Golly stood looking at her until he saw a rhythmic pulse in her neck. "Paul!" he said, and threw a bone-crushing right fist into his left palm. Then he walked out, leaving the door open.

Sandra lay there for over an hour, though she was not unconscious all that time. She reeled to her feet presently, with some vague notion of going to the telephone. Instead she went up to the bedroom and fell asleep there.

She dreamed. A horrible thing, in which Paul and Golly circled around her. Paul was smiling and Golly was grinning and what made it horrible was that neither of them was all there. They were half-men, sometimes the top half and sometimes the right and sometimes the left, and where the real part ended there was blood.

She tossed and screamed, and she burst out laughing and woke herself up. She rose and showered and went to bed again, sleeping very late.

The next day she called Paul Egan.

She spoke urgently, hurriedly, saying only that she wanted him, needed him. He agreed to come. When he arrived she was on the porch, waiting. She had been there a long time, looking down the road, a circle of words running through her mind, losing their meaning, losing everything but the power of hate they carried. Paul kills Golly kills Paul kills Golly kills Paul. . . .

It was dusk when he came. She caught his arm and drew him inside, reaching back for the switch of the hanging lamp in the foyer.

"You see, Paul? You see?"

He looked at the knobbed discoloration on her cheek and jaw and nodded. "The scum. The dirty scum. Why did he do it?"

"Because of you, Paul." She put her face in his shoulder, and his arms went around her, easily, quietly. "Paul, Paul, he's going to kill you."

Paul tightened his arms around her and then pressed her away. He shrugged out of his coat and hung it on the newel post. "When was he here?"

"Last night, early."

"I—had an idea." She wished she could see his face.

"You had? Paul, why didn't you come?"

He laughed a little. "Last time I was here you said you wanted no violence. Remember?"

"Yes. Well—I—got the violence. What are we going to do?"

"Have you any ideas?"

"I want him killed," she said dully, and cringed as if from herself. "Paul!" I didn't mean that! I— Oh, I don't know what I'm saying!"

"Killing him wouldn't be a way out," Paul said in a harsh voice. "We've got to—I've got—" He clutched his face, rocking his head back and forth. "If I could only know what he was doing—find out how he—"

"There can't be a showdown, if that's what you mean," she said, coming to him, comforting him. "He'd be on you like a snake."

"Oh no. You don't understand. He wouldn't work that way, no matter how direct and violent he seems to you. He'd figure something out cleverly, set a trap for me. He wouldn't—do anything to me directly."

"He's afraid of you!"

"Perhaps he is," whispered Paul. His upper lip was wet. "I can't stand any more of this, Sandra, I can't. We'll have to force his hand. If he once tries to kill me and fails, I don't think he'll ever come back. It's as far as he can go."

"Why? I don't see why. Why don't you find him? Why don't you have him arrested? What kind of a man are you—" her hand strayed to her bruised face— "that you can think of waiting for him to make the next move after *this?*"

He looked at her, and the twisted agony is his eyes wrung something within her. "Trust me, Sandra. I know what I'm up against. I tell you, if he tries and fails, you'll never see him again. I *know.* Trust me."

She took his hands. "He'll kill you."

"I think not. Not if I'm careful. Not if I watch every move I make. I know how he works. He will set some sort of trap somewhere where I do something regularly. I must do nothing quite the same until he tries to—to— Oh, Sandra! Why did this have to happen to you? I love you. You asked for none of this. Maybe it would be better if I went away and never—"

She closed his mouth with her hand. "I thought of that, Paul. Maybe I'm crazy —maybe something's wrong with me, I don't know; but nobody, nobody ever before was willing to risk being killed for me. You could run away and hide, but you're sticking to face it—for me. I'm not afraid."

There were no words in what they had to say to each other after that.

Later, he looked at his watch. "San, can you spend the night in town? I'll get a hotel reservation for you. You'll be quite safe. I'll have lunch with you, and dinner, and we'll go to a show. Then I'll bring you back here. He'll know, you see; and when we get back here tomorrow night, together, he'll try. I know him."

She rose. "You're sure, Paul?"

"I'm sure."

She ran to get her bag packed.

HE PHONED her, anxiously, at bedtime, and again the next morning. They had lunch together at the Criterion, and dinner at the Sable Antelope, and took in a show.

In the taxi on the way back to her house, they were tense and silent until she asked, "You think he will be there?"

He nodded. "He should be. He knows . . . he must know."

She moved closer to him, and after a moment said, "Paul, don't—kill him."

"It isn't likely that I would," he said gently.

"Don't. Not for his sake, but—"

He held her close. "I know. I know," he murmured.

The cab deposited them at the curb and droned away with its life and its lights. They stood breathless, listening.

"I'm scared," she whispered. She felt his noiseless chuckle.

"Sure sign you're normal," he answered. "Come on."

She held back, questioning his sudden decisiveness. He bent and kissed her swiftly, a gesture so tender that again she was joltingly reminded of Gollys' ruthlessness, and she gasped in terror, feeling Golly so close.

Paul held the gate open for her, and they tiptoed up the path. She would have mounted the steps, but he stopped her.

"This is the way we always come," he

reminded her. "We must not do anything the same. I know him, darling. Some habit-pattern, some little, usual thing I do —that's where he'll ambush me. I *know*, Sandra. Uh—have you a key to the kitchen door?"

She nodded, and they crept around the house. Once a twig cracked somewhere, and once a dog howled down the road, and both times they froze and stood for minutes, their nerves strumming.

"Be funny if Golly wasn't around here at all," Paul breathed.

"Oh, he is, I know he is!" Sandra half sobbed. "Oh, I wish we were inside!"

"Don't be frightened!" he said, shaking her a little. "As long as you stay close to me he'll do nothing. If he wanted to kill you he'd have done it the other night. It's me he's after. Hurry; open the door."

The key was annoyingly disobedient in her fingers, but she got the door open. She pulled him in and away from it and slid the bolt. Then she turned on the light and screamed at the looming bulk in the corner.

"Silly! It's just your raincoat!" Paul hissed.

It was, and the reaction was crushing. She clung to him, trembling.

When she had quieted, he spoke. "You're quite safe now, San. Turn out the light. I'll go. No one will see me slip out, it's so dark. I've outwitted him so far. If I can once get home, I can—lock myself in. But I wish he tries. I wish he tries to kill me, and fails. If he does, he will never come back."

"Oh Paul, I hope you're right! I hope you know what you're doing!" she cried.

"I do, darling. Truly I do. Trust me. And don't worry. I'll be careful. Good night, darling." He did not attempt to kiss her, and again she had that suffocating awareness of Golly's presence.

In the darkness he left her. A blacker piece of blackness, he glided out to the door and entered the garden.

She reshot the bolt, and ran to the front windows. She could just see him out there, stepping softly along the edge of the path, on the lawn, freezing suddenly as the willows rustled in the casual breeze.

After a long while he moved again, reached the gate, and instead of swinging it wide as he usually did, opened it only enough to let him slide through. He let it close, leaned back over it, and stared carefully all around him. Her eyelids strained in sympathy with his.

Then he stood erect, and with the old, endearing gesture, whipped off his hat and waved it high over his head. She smiled, and three jets of flame squirted toward him and he fell writhing to the sidewalk, his agonies drowning out the echoes of the gunshots.

It seemed to Sandra that he choked for a long, long time. Then she was conscious of the stillness and of the cramped

muscles in her cheeks, holding her smile, and of the other, sharper pain of the long splinter she had driven under her finger-nail when she clutched at the windowsill.

Then she walked to the telephone and called the police, and sat woodenly in the dark to wait.

THERE was a fatherly man who asked questions in a soft voice. He had point-ed gray eyebrows, and came after all the others, the ones who took Paul away and the ones with floodlights and flash-bulbs.

The fatherly man asked her all about Paul and Golly, and how long she had known them, and how she felt about them, and many questions about herself. She an-swered them all, the answers seeming to come only from the front of her face. She kept her hands over her eyes, and spoke dully from between the heels of her hands.

When he had stopped his questions, he thought for minutes, silently. She took her hands down then, and began her own questions.

"Where was he?"

"Who?"

"Golly, of course!"

He looked at her sadly.

"There was no one there but Paul."

"But the guns—"

"The guns were tied to the trees on each side of the path, and to the eaves of the house. There were strings from their triggers, knotted together over the gate. When he waved his hat—"

"He always did that."

"Of course. He knew that the attempt would be made around some accustomed action—and he forgot to change that one."

She tossed her head miserably from side to side. "I don't understand!"

The kindly man spread his hands.

"You've heard about the psychosis that sometimes affects twins, haven't you? The thing that makes one feel incomplete as long as the other exists?"

"I—suppose so."

"Well, this is just an extension of the same thing."

"But that's crazy!"

The man shook his head slightly. "Paul Egan wasn't exactly all there."

"Paul?"

"Paul, yes. Paul Egan, the man who murdered himself."

She sprang up. "But it was Golly! It was Golly who killed Paul!"

"Sandra—you don't mind if I call you Sandra?—can't I make you understand? There was only one of them."

"Oh, no. No. Golly was—"

"—was Paul. Be quiet, now, and listen to me. Paul Egan was what is called a 'dissociative personality.' Some people have three or four very strong and quite separate personalities. Paul's divided quite sharply and completely."

"But didn't he know?"

"He knew, all right—but the chances are that he never remembered what he did when he was Golly."

"Why didn't he tell me?" she whis-pered.

"He loved you, I suppose."

"Why did he let Golly—why did he take that chance?"

The man shrugged. "I can only guess. From what you tell me, I gather that he was convinced that 'Golly's' failure in a murder attempt would be the end of Golly in his life. He probably reasoned that for the 'Golly' personality to be caught in an effort to do away with himself would be such a shock that 'Golly' would never return."

"Golly and Paul," she murmured. "You're playing with me!" she flared. "I don't believe it! I won't! I won't!"

He caught her wrists, pressed her gent-ly back to her chair. "Listen to me, child. On the guns, on all of Golly's presents, on the tools that were used to make the booby-trap, and all over the house, are Paul Egan's fingerprints."

After a while, Sandra believed it.

SHOCKERS AHEAD

COOPER, the stolid, calm anaesthetist, checked pulse and respiration, then nodded briefly at Dr. Andre Spence. Andre felt fear and what was akin to self-loathing as he glanced at the placid sleeping face of Marianne. He dreaded this operation.

It was still not too late to change his mind. Cooper would be mildly surprised. Miss Watson, the phlegmatic surgical nurse, might lift one heavy eyebrow.

Andre was grateful for the protection of mask, cap, gown. He wondered if above the mask his eyes glittered strangely. Small wonder if they did.

The worst danger was that raw, reckless Bettinger would get wind of it, would come storming into the small operating theatre, blinded to everything except the love he bore the sleeping Marianne.

He stood by the table, looked down at the firm, fair forehead. Behind that plate of bone lay the frontal lobes. In those lobes there was the memory of his murder of his wife. Murder that used the unsuspecting Marianne as a tool.

He had no doubt but that what he was about to do was unparalleled in medical history, or any other kind of history. A murderer was about to open the brain case of the only witness to the crime, and remove therefrom all memory of that crime, thus making him forever safe.

Killing her would be simpler, of course —but that was unthinkable. Much as he dreaded operating on her, it was better than snuffing out her life. Yes, it was much better. He could not contemplate a world in which Marianne did not exist. She had been the reason for his wife's murder.

When he had finished the lobectomy, memory would be gone, and her personality would be slightly changed. A bit more extraverted perhaps. Maybe she wouldn't want to resume her position. But what need was there for her to work? He, Andre Spence, would keep her and protect her and love her all the days of his life.

His rubber-gloved hands were trembling. He stilled them with an effort. He would have to cease thinking of the patient as Marianne. She must become merely another case, his latest psycho-surgical patient.

Cooper and Watson were beginning to glance at him oddly, wondering, no doubt, why he didn't begin. How fortunate that her knowledge of his murderous guilt had given her that acute combination of fear, anxiety and uncertainty which enabled him to diagnose it as an organic lesion of the frontal lobe.

Scalpel in hand, he drew a red, double-looped line across her forehead, just below the hair line. He paused for the barest fraction of a second, then his lean strong hands began to work rapidly.

Stop! Was that a heavy, familiar step in the corridor? The steps went on. His hand trembled again.

A trickle of sweat stung his eye and he blinked it away. Scalpel in hand, he stared down, with increasing tension, at the delicate dura beyond which was the brain of Marianne.

The complete shocker will be told by John MacDonald in his novel—"No Grave Has My Love"—in the next issue, . . . out August 4th.

—The Editor.

VENOMOUS

Spine-Chilling Novelette of One Man's Nightmare

By John D. MacDonald

CHAPTER ONE

Whisper From the Past

THE city of Sayreton, Iowa—population 14,000—steamed and sweltered on the relentless hotplate of an airless August day. Peter Hume, blissfully cool in the small restaurant, thought longingly of a tall collins, of several tall collinses, stood up with regret and walked with his check to the cashier by the door.

"Terrible hot day. Mr. Hume," the girl said.

She dropped his change onto the green rubber mat and he picked it up. "I hate to go out into it, Helen."

She smiled at him. "When's the wedding, Mr. Hume?"

"Next Monday. Four days away."

"Miss Owen is a lovely girl, Mr. Hume. Where you going on the honeymoon?"

"Lake Louise."

Helen gave him a dreamy look. "Oh, baby!" she said softly.

Peter blushed and pushed the door open. The heat was like a steam bath.

●

Peter's past was dead—strangled with tortured memories of faraway Calcutta—until a malignant ghost returned with a soul of unquenchable hate.

LADY • • •

"Wanda thought I was trying to steal her boy-friend guard. . . ."

When he stepped off the curb, his heel seemed to sink into the asphalt. A day to fry eggs on the pavement. A day to sit in the tub.

He realized that if it weren't for the wedding coming up, he would be tempted to quit for the day. But he wanted to leave a clean desk behind him and there was a lot to do.

In his office building, he got out at the fifth floor, walked down the corridor and paused for a moment to admire the discrete gilt lettering on the opaque glass panel of the door.

Peter B. Hume
Attorney at Law

Whistling, he opened the door, threw his hat and grinned with satisfaction as it looped over the hook on the coat tree.

Robina Bray, seated at her desk in the outer office applauded languidly. "Hooray for dead-eye!"

She was a girl with rusty red hair and a spattering of freckles across the bridge of her nose. Her eyes were sea green. Her face was too long for beauty, her mouth too wide and her teeth too big. When, after his discharge three years before, he had returned to Sayreton and let it be known that he needed a secretary for his law office, she was the first one to appear.

He had asked her a few times about what she had done during the years since he had last seen her. They had been in high school at the same time. She had been a sophomore when he had graduated and gone away to school.

She made a few vague comments about working in New York. He found out from other sources that the man she had intended to marry had been killed overseas. She was a top-notch girl, an excellent secretary. She never told him why she had come back to Sayreton. In fact, he wondered why *he* had come back. Annaly Owen, no doubt.

Robina Bray's face was even a bit homely, but the rest of her was superb. Tall and broad shouldered, with long legs, a high slim waist, nice curves. She seemed continually and wryly amused by the combination of face and body, and wore clothes which accentuated her build.

After she had worked for him for eleven months, he had kissed her. He remembered it well. She had been getting ready to leave for the day. She had responded, warmly and quickly, and then moved away from him.

"No dice, Peter my lad. This is a small town. No dice at all. Once more and you get yourself a new secretary."

And that had been all.

He might have been tempted to try again, had not Annaly Owen appeared on the scene, fresh from college, five years younger than Peter's twenty-seven. Pale angel. Blonde hair like cobwebs in the moonlight, amethyst eyes. Soft gentle lips and a sweet gravity. Breathlessness in her voice.

Her father was a retired contractor. Her mother was dead. Annaly ran the house with a firm hand, which seemed strange in anyone so young, so soft, so melting. . . .

Peter unbuttoned the seersucker jacket and pulled his soaked shirt away from his skin. "Phooo," he said.

Robina Bray looked up at a lock of hair on her forehead. She stuck her lower lip out and blew it back. "Tomorrow I come in a swim suit. I warn you."

"It ought to increase the clientele, Robby."

"You say the sweetest things, boss. Robby has a surprise for you." She took a small, pale blue envelope from her desk. She held the envelope up to her nose, inhaled deeply, closed her eyes and said, "Ahhhh!"

He snatched it out of her hand. On the front of the envelope in jet black, tiny feminine handwriting, it said, *Peter Hume.*

He frowned. "That's not Annaly's handwriting!"

"That's what makes it so much fun! I found it under the door when I unlocked the joint after lunch."

He too smelled the envelope. It had a sharp clear scent, oddly exotic.

"Essence of Malayan orchids," Robina said.

It touched a half-forgotten memory. The room was suddenly cool. Peter Hume bit his lower lip, tore open the small envelope.

Peter, Darling:
I suggest that you come to see me in room 414 at the Sayreton House at precisely three this afternoon.
                                      Your
                                      Lynda

SWEAT was cold on the palm of his hand. He crumpled the note as though to throw it in the basket beside Robina, then shoved it into his coat pocket, turned and went into his office, slammed the door.

As in a dream, he walked around to the far side of his desk, slumped in the chair and looked at the far wall. It was incredible and unbelievable.

But it had happened. Oddly he felt that he had always known it would happen. He glanced at his watch. One twenty. One hour and forty minutes to go.

He sat and remembered the past. It came back with a rush of vividness that startled him.

Early 1944. He had been a service officer in the OSS detachment in Calcutta. Though he had volunteered for many missions, they thought too highly of him in a supply and administrative category to let him go. They had said many kind words to him, but in the end he was left in the midst of routine in Calcutta.

The worst of it was having nothing to do when the work was done.

Nothing until he found Lynda Stanley.

He was twenty-three at the time. She was thirty. By now she'd be thirty-four. She was in Calcutta working as a civilian with one of the information agencies.

There had been something intriguingly foreign about her. She was a small woman with jet black hair, dark eyes, a sallow skin. She had private means over and above her substantial salary, and lived with three servants in a small bungalow in the Tollygunge area. He had met her in a large party at Firpo's. She had been with a British major who had passed out early in the evening in a most dignified manner.

He had taken her home, had made a date for later in the week. They had gone to several movies together, more for the reason of taking advantage of the air conditioning than to see the pictures.

Her attitude toward him had been one of amusement. It had become a challege to him to take that look of amusement out of her eyes and replace it with something more flattering. He had tried to kiss her several times, but she had laughed at him.

One night she had invited him to a dance at the Tollygunge Club. To his surprise she began to drink rather heavily. They stayed until the dance was over and the other guests had gone home. They sat alone on the terrace in the moonlight. The moonlight glinted on the dark water in the swimming pool.

Suddenly she leaned over and kissed him. She looked up at him with challenge in her dark eyes. "What's the matter, big boy?" she asked softly. "You afraid of me?"

After that he saw her constantly. The faint look of amusement did not fade out of her eyes, but he was too far gone to care. Besides, when his mouth was pressed fiercely to hers, she could not laugh at him. . . .

She would never talk of herself. His infatuation grew rather than diminished.

At last, in spite of his efforts to avoid it, he was sent home on points for discharge. On the last night before he left she asked him, "Do you love me, Peter?"

"You know I do!"

"Here is a present for you, Peter. No, don't turn on the light to look at it. It is a ring with a star sapphire. Does it fit?"

It fit perfectly.

She said, "The ring is in part for being sweet and in part for doing me a favor."

"Anything, Lynda."

"When you leave me I will give you a box of K ration. You will take it back with you. You will carry it with other boxes of ration, but you will mark it in some way so you can tell which is the one I gave you. When you get to the States, you will wrap it up and send it by parcel post to this address, which you will memorize. Say it after me: Gerald Rhine, P. O. Box 812, Jersey City, New Jersey."

He repeated it after her and said, "But I don't understand? What's in—"

"Part of the favor is in not asking questions, my darling. . . . It's a full ten minutes since I've been kissed."

Down the river from Calcutta to the sea and down to Trincomalee and over to Perth; then to Pearl and L.A. The box was with him. With every tossing mile of open sea that widened between the fantail of the APA and the Calcutta dock, the spell of Lynda Stanley grew less. And the curiosity about the package increased. Gems? Possibly.

Two days out of Los Angeles, he sat on the edge of his bunk and carefully undid the waxed ends of the package. It was filled with a fine, white, crystaline powder. He removed a pinch of it, heated the wax with his cigarette lighter and resealed the package.

HE TASTED one grain of the powder. It had no particular taste. He remembered stories he had read and, taking the slightest pinch on the back of his hand, sniffed it up his nostrils. After several minutes, a great warm wave of comfort and exhilaration swelled over him. He wanted to sing. He felt three times life size and capable of putting his naked fist through the steel hull next to his bunk.

He could remember the funniest stories he had ever heard, and could make up even funnier ones. He could write a great novel, or a wonderful song. Then all things swam away from him, and he seemed to be growing to an enormous size. He stretched out in the bunk and he could not tell when thought stopped and dreams started.

He didn't awaken until the next morning. He felt washed out and jaded. There was a cottony taste in his mouth.

He did a lot of thinking the rest of the trip. He thought of Lynda and how she had led him on, and he thought of the stuff he was supposed to smuggle in. He lay awake cursing her for the way she had used him.

After debarkation he asked to talk to the Port Commander. He annoyed a lieutenant, a captain and an elderly major by refusing to discuss his business with them. After a six hour wait, he was permitted to see the colonel.

After listening to the first three sentences, the colonel stopped him and made two phone calls. Twenty minutes later, two brisk young men in well-tailored suits showed up and Peter Hume was permitted to tell the entire story. A stenotype was brought in and finally, at midnight, the complete statement was ready for Peter's sworn signature.

They took the box and took his fingerprints. They put him up at a good hotel and assigned a man to stay with him. The next morning they told him that he could rejoin his shipment for discharge.

No, it will not be necessary for you to appear at the trial, Captain. We appreciate your informing us. You have done a very fine thing, Captain. Yes, we will keep your name out of it if possible. Thank you very much. Yes, we have mailed the box. Good-by and good luck, Captain.

During the three years since his discharge, memories of Lynda had faded. He forgot exactly what she looked like. But he could remember her smile and the smell of her dark, shoulder-length hair.

And he could remember the perfume with which the blue note had been scented.

Your Lynda!

His office door opened and Robina stood in the doorway. "Trouble, boss?"

He nodded. She pursed her lips. "The past is rearing its ugly head?"

"Something like that."

"From the smell of the billy doo, chum, she is something spectacular. And, as I told you some time ago, thees Fon du Lac, she ver' small town, Musseer. Better stick the fair Annaly's head in a sack until the ex does a dust."

Peter smiled grimly. "It's not so simple, Robby."

"Then, my boy, you've had it."

"I wish I could tell somebody about it."

Robina walked in, sat down in the visitor's chair, crossed very lovely legs and said, "Try me."

"I can put it in one sentence: While I was overseas I made an ass of myself over an American gal seven years older than me who, when we parted, gave me this ring and a box to smuggle into the states—but I opened the box, found narcotics and turned her in when I arrived in L.A."

Robina Bray's sea green eyes widened and her eyebrows climbed up toward her rusty hair. "And this is the dish? The note came from her?"

He nodded. Robina whistled softly. "She wants to see you, no doubt."

"At three. At the Sayreton House."

Robina tilted her head on one side and stared at Peter with a speculative look. "She has a legitimate gripe, you know."

"How so?"

"If you didn't want to get your little fingers all dirtied up with smuggling, you could have dropped the nasty old box over the side."

Peter nodded. "I thought of that. Then I remembered how I thought all the time I knew her that she was laughing at me. And I thought of all the other suckers who would be used to bring the stuff in. . . .

"I've seen snowbirds, you know. I've seen them when they couldn't stop yawning and when they batted at the empty air in front of their noses, trying to chase away flies that weren't there. I've seen them sweat and moan and shake when they're off the stuff. Not pretty, Robby. Not pretty at all, at all. And if I had chucked the box over the side, she would

have angled somebody else into bringing the next package."

"So you turned her in," Robby said.

Peter stood up, flushed and angry. "Damn it, Robby, she was playing me for a sucker! Depending on her charm to keep me from messing with that box she gave me."

"And especially you didn't like being laughed at?"

His anger faded. He managed to grin at her. "Maybe that's closer, lady."

Robina stood up. "I still love you, Peter my lad. Be on your guard. One would suspect that she means you no good."

She closed the door behind her and Peter put his head on the desk, his cheek on the back of his right hand. The light came through the blinds, and the six points of the perfect star in the sapphire ring sparkled. He yanked the ring off and dropped it into his desk drawer.

CHAPTER TWO

Hot Eyes of Hate

ROOM 414 was at the end of the corridor. His footsteps made no sound on the thick corridor rug. His mouth felt tight and dry.

He lifted his hand, took a deep breath and knocked on the dark door. It was two minutes after three. A familiar, throaty voice said, "Come in, Peter darling."

His hand was cold and wet on the knob. He opened the door. It opened into a small sitting room. Beyond was the bedroom. Lynda Stanley stood at the window, looking down into the court. She wore a house coat of pale blue taffeta. She was much thinner than she had been in Calcutta.

She turned away from the window. For a moment she was silhouetted against the light and he couldn't see her face. She walked toward him, hands outstretched.

"How nice to see you, Peter," she said softly.

"Nice to see you, Lynda," he mumbled.

She took his hands and turned so that the light struck her face. An ugly puckered scar started by the lobe of her left ear and slashed down across her cheek. It disappeared and then reappeared low on her throat, disappearing into the top of the house dress.

She knew he was looking at it. He licked dry lips.

"Pretty, isn't it, Peter?"

Her voice was still soft. He looked into her dark eyes. They were like dull chips of black marble. Lifeless, dead, ugly and completely mad. He felt the skin on the back of his neck prickle.

"What—what happened to you?" he asked.

"Oh, it was a present from you, Peter. A lovely present from my lovely little man, my brave and righteous little man."

"I don't underst—"

She let go of his hands and traced the angry, puffy scar with one finger.

"See, Peter. It was a girl named Wanda something or other. She was in there because she had killed her two children. Poor thing, she had wanted to go away with a pleasant truck driver and the children were in the way. Horrid place, that prison. She worked beside me in the laundry. See my hands, Peter. A three-year sentence. I served two and a half years in the laundry. Do you think the swollen knuckles will ever go down? Red and cracked, aren't they?"

"Look, I—"

"Don't you want to hear about it, Peter? Wanda thought I was trying to steal her boy-friend guard. . . . She took a pair of scissors from the tailor shop and walked up to me and slashed me. She had the general idea of removing an eye, but I ducked."

Her cheeks were faintly hollow and the new thinness of her face made her dark, dead eyes look unnaturally enormous.

She stepped closer to him, her lips parted and said, "But I'm still attractive to you, aren't I, Peter?"

He saw the bottle on the table by the window. He smelled the rye on her breath. With a quick stride, he reached the bottle, twisted the top off, tilted it up to his lips, swallowed deeply and nearly gagged on the tepid whiskey.

He sat down on the small couch. "Lynda, I can't tell you how sorry I am. I—what do you want?"

"Why, I wanted to see you, Peter!"

"But what can I—"

"I wanted to thank you for the favor you did me. You had to save the world from such a nasty, unpleasant woman, didn't you?"

She sat beside him, half facing him. She giggled. "I should be on the other side of you, darling. Then the scar wouldn't show so much."

Peter had never felt so terrible in his life. He didn't know what to say.

She leaned her cheek against his shoulder and smiled up at him. The dark eyes were full of hate, and as dead as two lumps of coal. But she smiled. The scar was lurid and the closeness of it made his stomach turn over.

"Remember how you told me you loved me, Peter?" she asked softly. "You still love me, don't you, Peter? Take me in those strong arms of yours. You can draw the shades and the scar won't show."

"You've had your fun," a new voice said. A male voice. Peter spun around quickly and saw a man leaning against the door frame. He must have been standing in the bedroom listening to the conversation.

HE WAS anything but impressive—a smallish man with an oval gray face, sparse brown hair, faded blue eyes, a nose like a damp cruet. His voice was thin and tired. The brightest spot of color in his face was an oversized underlip which sagged away from small pointed teeth. The lip was purplish red, mottled and swollen. He wore an oxford gray suit which looked much too thick and warm for the day, but he didn't appear to be sweating. His skin looked dry and dusty.

He licked a good third of a cigarette and put it carefully in the middle of his mouth. He lit it and left it there. It flapped as he said, "You've had your fun, Lynda. Let's get down to business."

Lynda crossed the room and sat on a chair facing Peter.

"Who are you?" Peter asked.

"Call me Miss Stanley's manager, Hume."

"What kind of business have you got with me?" Peter demanded.

The man began to count on tiny white fingers. "One is the house on South Walker Street. Number 809. When your father died two years ago, he left it to you. It'll bring fifteen thousand cash money on the open market, more if we had time to play around. Two is the farm on the Mill Road. Two hundred and forty acres. Twenty-five thousand quick money. Three is the big four-hundred-acre place ten miles north of town. The one your grandpappy started. It's worth forty thousand in a quick sale if its worth a dime. Four is a small mortgage on your office furniture and fixtures. Your credit is good. Throw in your car and you can get a thousand.

"Five is your prospective father-in-law. He has large bills tucked away. He'll make a loan of five thousand without any questions. Give him a mysterious line about a wonderful opportunity you can't discuss yet. The whole amount comes to the grand total of eighty-six thousand bucks. We'll give you exactly one week to get it all together, and we want it in cash. Small used bills, nothing bigger than a fifty. You may have to drive up to Des Moines to secure some of it."

Peter sat very still. He looked at his knuckles. He fingered the smooth place on his finger where the sapphire ring had worn the hair from it.

He said, "And why should I pay you eighty-six thousand dollars?"

"Compensation for Lynda's injuries. Time spent in the can. For shooting off at the mouth."

"I won't pay you a dime," Peter said.

The man laughed. "Look, brother. You don't know what a break you're getting. Lynda over there is real sore at you. You know what she wanted to do? She wanted me to hire some punk to come down here and fill you with hot lead. She wanted me to spend good syndicate money to maybe have you snatched and have you taken apart slow with a dull knife. But I don't go for that kind of thing. I play it fair and square. We get the eighty-six thousand and we leave you alone."

Peter shook his head. This couldn't be happening in the clean little Iowa city of Sayreton, population 14,000. He said, "You're wasting your time. I don't scare easily."

The man laughed again and said, "You know, she even asked me if we could cross you up and take the dough and then spray a little acid across the face of that pale babe of yours. But I told her, I said, 'Lynda, when Archy Krakow makes a bargain with a guy, he don't cross him up before it's over.' You got to understand, guy, that Lynda is real mad at you.

"Now you take the syndicate. Hell, they're not mad. We spent good money getting Lynda planted in that overseas slot so she could handle shipments for us. You ratting on her was just one of the breaks of the game. We don't hold a grudge. But Lynda's different. She takes it personal."

Peter looked over at Lynda and then looked quickly away. An avid desire for his death was plain in her eyes. But it was the thought of what might happen to Annaly that really got him.

"Suppose I don't want to pay," Peter said.

"Guy, I hope you're just asking out of curiosity," Krakow said. "Just as a teaser, I might have Lynda go to your house, tear her dress and scratch herself up a little and then phone the cops. This is a small town, Pete. People don't go for that sort of stuff."

"This is extortion. There are laws against it."

Krakow licked another cigarette. "Call the cops, guy. Lynda is an old overseas pal of yours. No harm in looking you up, is there? You just want to give her a little present, guy. Eighty-six thousand bucks. Let her pick out her own present."

"It's only money," Lynda said hoarsely. "It's not enough. I hope he doesn't pay. I hope he tries to get wise."

"Shut up," Krakow said gently.

Lynda stood up and her mouth was a thin, tight line. She walked over to Peter, looked down at him and said, "I told myself every night for nearly three years, Peter, that one day I'd watch you roll on the floor and scream. I might still do that, you know. I might do something worse."

She went into the bedroom, pushing by Krakow, slamming the door behind her.

Krakow smiled sleepily. "You got her real mad, guy. And she was a snowbird once before the syndicate had her cured." He tapped his forehead. "Gotta watch those snowbirds. They get the cure, but they aren't always okay up here. Get me?"

Peter stared at his clenched fists.

Krakow said, "Don't take it so hard, guy. It's only money. I'll keep her from marking up your bride. But don't go to the cops, or I'll turn her loose. She doesn't give a damn if she burns for murder. She's pretty sore about losing her looks. You know how woman are."

Peter rose. "I'll have to think about it."

Krakow sighed. "You got no thinking to do, guy. You got to spend your time raising money. Run along, now. We'll be in touch. You want to get hold of me, I'm in 413, right across the hall."

PETER walked numbly out into the corridor. The door slammed behind him. He went down in the elevator and walked out and got behind the wheel of his car. If they had not known everything about him, he would have had more confidence. He knew the valuations Krakow had placed on his property were accurate to the last dollar.

He sat stupidly behind the wheel of the car, his sweating hands on the steering wheel. The whole scene made him think of tense movies he had seen. Murder and death. Then you walk out of the darkness of the movie and there you are in the bright afternoon sunshine, blinking at the everyday street scenes, grinning a little because the movie had somehow made you think that you were going to walk out into a damp and foggy night where a dark figure waited for you in an alcove.

But this was three-forty in the afternoon in Sayreton and what went on up in Room 414 wasn't a movie. He thought of Annaly and shivered.

He put the key in the ignition, started the motor and drove out into traffic without looking. Tires screamed on the asphalt and somebody yelled at him. He shook his head to clear it and tried to concentrate on his driving.

Minutes later he put the car in the lot, rode up in the elevator and walked into his office. Robina stopped typing and looked up at him. She stared at him for a moment, then pushed her chair back and hurried to him.

"Peter!" she said. "You're ill!"

He smiled feebly and shook his head. "I'm not sick. Just—upset."

He went on into his own office, leaving the door open. She came in and closed the door. She had a paper cup and a pint bottle.

She poured a stiff jolt and handed it to him. His hand shook as he lifted it to his lips. The liquor had a wet cardboard taste from the paper cup. It burned his throat.

She sat beside the desk and looked anxiously at him. "What happened?"

"She had a friend with her. They want a little money. She was in prison for two and a half years. She was hurt. Bad scar."

"I didn't like the way you said 'a little money'."

"All I can borrow, plus all I have."

"Shall I get Chief Daniels on the phone?" She reached for the phone on his desk.

He caught her wrist. "No!"

"Why not?" she asked, puzzled.

"Robby, she's mad. Absolutely insane. Some syndicate or other put her in that overseas spot to handle shipments to this country. Right now they're using her madness to get money out of me.

"But she isn't interested in money. She wants me dead. If I don't play ball, they'll just turn her loose on me. She's of no use to them at anything else in her current condition. It's as though you were in a yard and a man had a vicious dog on a chain, and he told you to throw him your purse or the dog might get away from him. What would you do?"

Robina leaned back in the chair and bit her lips. "How about getting police protection and telling them to go to hell?"

In a low voice Peter said, "They know about Annaly. They said something about acid. She'd like to throw acid on Annaly. She hates every woman that isn't scarred like she is." He shook his head hopelessly. "You didn't see her, Robby. You didn't see the way her eyes look. Dead. Like the coal on top of a furnace fire after it's been banked. There's fire underneath, but you can't see it. Yet you know it can blaze up!"

"Hey," she said. "Take it easy!"

He cupped his palms over his eyes, his short fingernails digging deeply into his hairline.

"Peter, you must have turned her in to federal officers."

He nodded.

"Then maybe they can give you protection."

For a moment he felt a surge of hope. Then it faded. "What have they got on her to warrant picking her up? I couldn't take a chance. In ten minutes of freedom she could ruin Annaly's life. I'll have to pay."

Robina set her jaw. "I'd fight! I wouldn't let them get away with it."

"I made a mistake and I've got to pay for it."

"Nuts! This baby was a grown-up girl. She was having her fun. Don't go all soft and sorry on me, my lad."

"I've got to pay them," he said.

He took out his cigarettes. She took one and he lit hers and his own. His hand was a bit steadier.

She slouched so that her rusty hair was against the top edge of the back of the chair. She looked up at the plaster ceiling while she slitted her eyes and blew a fat, slow smoke ring.

After a moment she said, "Peter, why don't you tell Annaly the whole situation? Tell her what danger she's in. Send her away. Send her up to Des Moines and have her register under some other name. Or drive her up yourself. Daniels will give you a permit to carry a gun. Come on back here and tell them all to go to hell."

He thought it over. It seemed all right except for one detail. There was no point in explaining that detail to Robina. He sighed. "I'll try it, Robby."

She stood up and grinned at him. "Now you're my boy. Run along and I'll brush off the clients that are swarming in the outer office, I hope."

CHAPTER THREE

Annaly the Golden

ANNALY'S heels made firm clacking sounds on the parquet floor as she walked down the hall to the screen door. Her pale hair, which Peter liked better at shoulder length, the ends curled softly inward, was piled high on her head, giving her a look of fragility, emphasizing the slender and delicate contour of her throat.

"Why Peter!" she said, pushing the screen door open. "What are you doing here at this time of day? I thought you had work to do." She wore a crisp cotton dress, smooth and tight around her tiny waist. Her lips were coral pink and soft.

She was a haven, a place of refuge, a place of forgetfulness. He took her hungrily in his arms, kissed the side of her throat just under her ear, and then her lips.

With the warm breathlessness he loved, she pushed him away. "Really, darling!" she said, laughing.

"Is your father around?"

"He's in the upstairs study. Do you want to see him?"

"No. I want to talk to you."

"I have a guest. . . ."

"Send her away, darling. This is important."

Annaly shrugged and led the way down the hall to the drawing room. Peter gave a start of surprise as he saw the tall young man standing by the fireplace.

"Peter, I want you to meet Jimmy Cowl. Peter Hume." Her voice was high, slightly nervous. "Jimmy was taking graduate work at Harvard when I was at Wellesley, Peter. He worked for the State Department."

James Cowl was blond and tanned and thick through the shoulders. His gabardine suit was steel gray. His handshake was firm.

"Always glad to meet bridegrooms," he said. There was a faint undercurrent in his tone that Peter couldn't quite understand, but his voice was hearty and open.

"Surprise visit?" Peter asked.

"In a way. I've always threatened to drop in on Annaly. Haven't I?" he said, turning to her.

"That's right," she said cheerfully. "Jimmy, Peter has something he wants to talk to me about. Would you be a dear and take your drink out onto the back terrace for a little while. Right through that door there."

James Cowl smiled pleasantly, picked up a tall cool drink and walked out of the room.

Annaly frowned at Peter. "Now what is so horribly important, darling?"

He sat down heavily. She stood over him, her hands on her hips and looked down at him. It wasn't the time or the place for the story he had planned to tell. His mind raced. He said:

"Annaly, honey, some people have arrived in town. You know I was in OSS during the war. Well, I was forced to make trouble for them. They've come to get even with me somehow, and I'm worried about you. I think it would be a good thing if you left town for a while. A week, maybe."

Her hand went to her throat. "But the wedding, Peter! What could they do to me? Would—would they want to hurt me? But that's ridiculous!"

"They know the wedding is in four days, honey, and they've got us over a barrel. We might have to skip it. Postpone it."

Her eyes widened. "But what about you, darling? If I went away, wouldn't they try to do something to you?"

He reached up and pulled her down into his lap. She turned, and was light and warm against him, her face in the hollow of his neck and jaw. Her coral lips were touching his as she murmured, "At this point I should say, 'But Peter! It's only afternoon!'"

He held her fragile warmth tightly and thought that should anything happen to her, there would be nothing left to live for.

Despite the heat, he shivered.

"These people are dangerous," he said.

"But this is our own city. Full of our friends. . . . Are they really dangerous?"

He remembered the look in Robby's eyes as she had said, "I'd fight!"

In the quiet room the threat of Lynda seemed far away. Yet this girl was too important to take chances with.

"I can buy them off," he said.

"Buy them off!"

"It will mean that I'll have to get rid of the property I own. And go into debt. We won't be as well fixed as we had planned."

SHE sat up on his lap, touched her fingertips to her pale hair, looking oddly like a little girl who had just been denied an ice cream cone. She gave him a quick, alert look.

"What have you done, darling?"

"What? I don't—"

"Oh, come now, Peter! My goodness! I know the sound of blackmail. If they want money, it means that you've done something you shouldn't. If it weren't that way, you could go to the police."

He looked at her miserably. "It isn't exactly that way, honey. There was a woman overseas and—"

She quickly slid out of his lap, no expression on her face, turned and put her cool fingertips against his lips.

"Don't tell me about it," she said, "I hadn't planned on marrying an angel, you know. I don't want to hear anything about her. I hate her already. Just tell these people, whoever they are, that the Mrs. Hume-to-be far prefers her husband to hang onto his money, and that she won't be upset by anything they can tell her."

"But you don't—"

"Hush, darling. I know about blackmail. You run along and don't worry. And don't try to frighten me into going out of town so that they can't tell me these horrid things about your past. If I get any letters that look odd, I'll give them to you unopened. If I get any phone calls from strangers, I'll hang up. And I won't talk to anyone I don't know. You go back and work hard, like a dear." She pushed him gently toward the front hall.

The screen door slammed behind him. As he went down the steps, he looked back to wave at her through the screen. But she was already gone.

He was back at the office at quarter to five. Robina's raised right eyebrow was a question mark. He stopped by her desk and said, "Get me Tom Wenther on the phone."

"He buys. . . . Peter, you're not going to—"

"Get me Tom Wenther!"

He slammed the door to his private office. When Wenther was on the line he said, "Tom, you still interested in my house?"

"Not particularly, Pete."

"Sacrifice, Tom. Eighteen thousand cash deal. On the line."

Wenther laughed. "Pete, it's too hot for humor. Every time I laugh I start sweating again. On a cash deal I'd give you twelve. Not a penny more."

"Split the difference?"

Wenther coughed dryly. The line was silent. "Deal for fifteen cash," Wenther said. "We'll fix up the papers tomorrow. Meet me at the bank at eleven."

"How about the Mill Road farm? Cash deal. Make an offer?"

"Pete, boy, are you in trouble?"

"I need the money for a hot investment."

"You sound more like a guy who has made an investment that wasn't so hot. Try Murray Graham. See you tomorrow." The line clicked and was dead.

Before he hung up, Robina, on the same line said, "Shall I get Murray Graham for you?"

"Immediately."

Murray Graham was oily and slick and careful. He had cleaned up during the war and was putting large bundles of cash into farm properties when the price was right.

He haggled and whined and finally made a tentative offer of sixty-six thousand· for the two farms, but refused to make any offer for either of them separately. Peter accepted the offer and Graham promised cash in five days.

AFTER he hung up, he sat with his face in his hands, his elbows on the desk. Robina came in slowly, stood looking at him. He lifted his face and gave her a weak smile.

"I take it the bride wouldn't cooperate?"

"No, Robby."

"So you're letting the ex have her way?"

"Not a flattering way to put it, Robby. I can't take chances with Annaly. I'd never forgive myself if anything happened to her. Money isn't very important when you weigh it against some things."

"Where will you live?"

"The Wintons are leaving one of the upstairs apartments. We can rent it from Tom."

"This is going to make Annaly very happy."

"She'll get used to it. I'll get the money back."

"In no less than fifteen years, chum. Let me see—Annaly will be thirty-seven at that point."

"What are you trying to prove?"

"That love may be blind, but it can still add."

"What have you got against Annaly?"

Her sea green eyes got very round. "Why nothing, Peter! How can you say such a horrid thing to poor little me?" She went out and slammed the door behind her.

After dark that night Peter walked the night streets of Sayreton. The voices of the children at play under the big elms were shrill. An ice cream man tinkled his interminable bell. He had a date with Annaly, but he called up and said that he couldn't make it. She replied that it was all right with her because she didn't feel well. It was a short cool conversation.

A million locusts sang in the trees and the fields. In the swamp near the edge of town the peepers made shrill chorus. Once he stopped, doubled his fist and slammed it against a tree between the sidewalk and the curb. All it did was hurt his knuckles. It didn't make him feel any better.

The next day he signed the proper papers and transferred the fifteen thousand into his account. He worked quietly and moodily in his office. Robina had little to say. The day was as depressingly hot as Thursday had been.

Karkow phoned at one fifteen. His thin, tired voice was low and confidential. "You're playing this real smart, guy."

"What do you mean?"

"A deed was recorded at noon over at the courthouse. I got a glimpse of the tax stamps. Fifteen. You got time to get it out of the bank. Bring it on over as a down payment, guy."

"When?" Peter asked weakly.

"Soon as you can make it. Get the cash and put it in a brown paper bag. I'll be up in my room." He hung up.

Peter walked blindly down to the bank, wrote out a check for the fifteen thousand. The cashier looked at him peculiarly as he said, "Small bills. Nothing more than a fifty."

"Trouble, Mr. Hume?"

"Of course not! Do as you're told!"

"Sure, Mr. Hume. Sure."

He shoved the bills into his briefcase, walked back up to the office. With the door shut, he transferred them to a brown paper bag.

He heard a soft step behind him and half turned before his head exploded into fragments and he fell down through unending space into blackness.

He came to on the floor, stretched out on his back. Somebody was bathing his forehead with cool water. He opened his eyes, winced and reached up to touch the lump over his ear.

Robina smiled down at him and said, "Good morning, morning glory."

He struggled up to a sitting position. "Somebody hit me!"

"The heat hit you, Peter. Heat stroke, I guess. I went down the hall for a minute. When I came back I found you on the floor. You'd keeled over and hit your head on your desk on the way down."

"Brown paper bag!" he gasped.

"Say, are you off your wagon?"

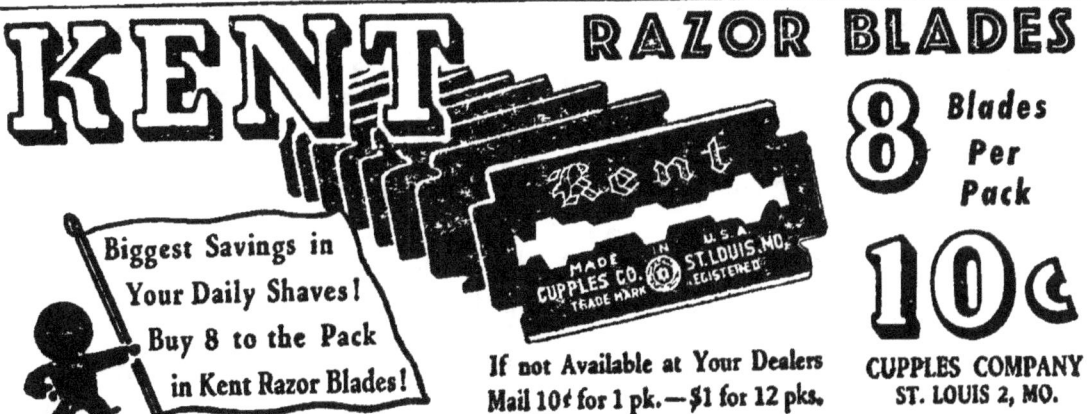

He lurched to his feet, wavered dizzily. "Where is it?"

"Where is what?"

"The brown paper bag!"

It was completely and definitely gone. He sat down heavily behind his desk. In a dull tone he asked, "Did you see anyone leave the office?"

"Didn't see anyone come or go."

"Robby, that bag had fifteen thousand dollars in it."

Her mouth was a round O.

"I was supposed to take it over to—her."

"What do you do now?"

"I've got to go tell Krakow. He's the man with her. He's expecting me."

CHAPTER FOUR

Nightmare

KRAKOW opened the door to 413, his right hand out of sight behind the door. He sighed, said, "Come in, guy. Where's the bag?"

He stuffed a small blue-black automatic pistol back under the oxford gray suitcoat. It went into place with an audible click.

"I haven't got the bag. I haven't got the money," Peter said hopelessly.

"Leave us not have fun and games, guy. This is a town I want to get out of. Maybe you'd like Lynda to go calling on Miss Owen this afternoon?"

"I had it all ready. I swear it. I had my back to the office door. Somebody came in and hit me. See the lump?"

Krakow jabbed the lump with the tip of his finger. "So that's the angle, guy? Not good, my friend. Not good. That won't save you either the dough or a lot of trouble."

"But I tell you somebody slugged me and took it!"

Krakow looked at him for five slow seconds and then said softly, "You know, I can almost believe you. Yes, I do."

His small white fist whipped up and smashed against Peter's mouth. Peter staggered but didn't fall. He lowered his head and started toward Krakow. The gun appeared in the man's hand. "Go sit down on the bed, guy. Honest, I could lick you, but it would take a little time and you might mark me. Sit down."

Peter sat on the bed, dabbed at his lips with his handkerchief and looked dully at the spots of blood on the white linen.

"That was for being careless," Krakow said. "Who knows the whole story?"

"Nobody but you and me and Lynda."

"Oh, come now. How about the beautiful Annaly?"

Peter shook his head.

"How about that redheaded crow in your office?"

"She doesn't know anything."

"What kind of phone setup you got in there?"

"A phone on her desk and a PBX on mine."

Krakow sighed. "Maybe I was careless. Maybe I ought to give you a poke at me. But I won't. Our baby is the redhead. She heard you on the phone. What's her name?"

"Robina Bray."

The door swung violently open. Krakow spun toward it, the gun still in his hand. Lynda stood and looked at Peter. She merely looked at him. But it made his mouth dry and tightened the muscles in his back and shoulder.

She wore the same taffeta housecoat. One hand was half hidden in the folds of the skirt. She smiled widely, an idiot smile. She took small mincing steps toward Peter. The room was very still. He heard the distant sounds of traffic on the street outside the hotel, the drip of a tap in the small bathroom.

Her lips pulled away from her teeth and she lunged at Peter, small nail scissors clenched in her hand. She drove them toward his eyes. Even as he rolled back away from her, he heard a thudding sound. She fell limply and rolled off onto the floor. The nail scissors were on the counterpane beside him.

Krakow shut the room door. He had slapped her across the temple with the barrel of the automatic. She lay on her back, her eyes shut, breathing heavily through her open mouth.

"See the trouble I've got?" Krakow said. "Her room door is open. Open this one and take a look at the hall. If it's clear, let me know."

The hallway was clear. "Okay," Peter said.

Krakow picked her up easily. Peter stood aside. Krakow grinned. "After you, guy. Always after you."

Inside Lynda's room, Krakow threw her roughly onto the couch, brushed his hands together and said, "I got her clothes locked up, but I don't know how long I can keep her off your neck. She's worse since she saw you yesterday."

Peter licked his lips. "What's going to keep her from coming back here after you take her away?"

"The syndicate keeps bargains, guy. You pay off and no trouble. She won't be back."

"How do I know that?"

"You don't. I take her back to the coast and put her back on the snow and then we unload her on a friend. The snow will keep her in line." He chuckled. "Old Lynda will probably wind up in one of those peep-hole joints in Cairo or Shanghai."

Peter swallowed thickly. He looked at the thin, beaten, unconscious woman on the couch and thought of the way she had looked in Calcutta. He thought of the yellow evening gown she had worn, of the way she had looked in the moonlight.

Krakow sighed. "There's the phone. Tell that Robina chicken of yours to get herself over here, but quick."

"No!" Peter said.

"Stop being an eagle scout! I'm not going to kill her."

Slowly, Peter walked to the phone, got the number.

"Peter Hume's office. Miss Bray speaking."

Hoarsely, "This is Peter."

"Yes?"

"I wonder if you could come over to the Sayreton House right away, *Robi*na."

"Oh! You can't talk."

"Right."

"And the way you said my name. It's about the robbery?"

"Room 414, Robina. And you might as well bring along the papers on the Daniels case. I'll sign them here and you can mail them in the lobby on your way out."

He hung up. Krakow grinned. "Still a cutey pants, hey? Daniels is the chief of police here. So she comes with cops?"

LYNDA stirred and sat up, slid her feet down onto the floor. She didn't say a word. She merely began to stare at Peter again. She ignored the trickle of blood that began to dry on her cheek. Her dark hair was tangled. She made no effort to smooth it back.

Krakow took a key out of his pocket and threw it to her. It landed in her lap. She kept looking at Peter.

"Your clothes are locked in my closet, Lynda. There's the key. Go get dressed. Maybe you've got work to do."

"No!" Peter said.

Krakow grinned. "Shut up, guy. You stopped having anything to do with this the minute you said the name Daniels."

Lynda walked out of the room and across the hall. Krakow lit a cigarette. Time passed slowly. Time of nightmare. "What are you going to do?" Peter asked.

Krakow yawned. "I'm tired of you and sick of this filthy little town. I'm going to grab back the fifteen thousand and leave. The hell with it. You crossed me up and I cross you up. Lynda is your problem.

When she gets dressed, I'll save her to turn loose on your redheaded crow if I have to. You just aren't smart, junior."

Through bloodless lips Peter said, "What about the police?"

"In the first place, they'll cover the joint, front and rear. They'll send this Robina up with the hick cop idea that if she doesn't show in fifteen minutes, they come up after her. They haven't got enough to go on to come up here with her. I think I can talk her into telling them it was all a big mistake and to please go away now."

"You seem pretty confident about what they'll do."

"After a few years you get to know how they think." He held up his hand and listened to the distant clang of an elevator door. "That'll be baby. You let her in when she knocks."

There was a hesitant knock on the door. Peter turned the knob to open it. As soon as the catch was released, the door crashed in at him, driving him violently back.

As he fell, he rolled, catching one quick glimpse of Krakow's contorted face. The automatic made a thin crack which was swallowed up by the harsh and heavy boom of a heavier gun.

Peter looked up at Krakow. The small man sagged back against the wall and grinned foolishly. His knees bent and he slowly slid down so that he was sitting on his heels. He coughed once, almost apologetically.

"Told them this was a lousy idea," he said to Peter. "Fooled me. Redhead fooled me. Private talent. Didn't know—had—any around. It is to laugh."

He coughed again, gave a start of surprise and agony, and slid over onto his side, blood frothing in the corner of his mouth.

Peter scrambled up. A wide young man with a dark, bitter face holstered the thirty-eight he held in his big hand. He gave a casual glance at Peter, walked in and dropped heavily onto one knee beside Krakow.

"Too good," he said softly.

Peter turned toward the door, saw the startled face of Chief Daniels and the taut, alarmed face of Robina Bray.

Daniels said in his high fussy voice, "You're perfectly all right. I heard the first shot. He fired the first shot. Self-defense."

Peter hurried to Robina, took her hands in his. She was shaking.

"I was afraid you were hurt, Peter. It would have been my fault. Last night I got these men by phone in Des Moines and hired them. They're—investigators. I gave them the whole story before I came to work this morning. When you got the call from this man, I phoned them. I told them to use their own judgment. They took the money."

The one who fired the shot said, "I'm Regan. Don't fret about the dough, Hume. We've got it all intact to hand back to you."

Suddenly Peter remembered Lynda. He looked beyond Robina, saw the door to 413 ajar, ran to it and flung it open. The room was empty!"

He turned to Reagan. "The woman—she's insane. Annaly! She's gone after Annaly!"

"Relax, Hume," Regan said. "I brought along one of our boys and posted him at your girl's house. Sorry I had to clip you. I thought it would bring things out in the open."

Peter said, "We better get over there. Fast!"

"Sure, Hume. Sure. But Miss Owen's okay. I guarantee it."

Regan, Robina and Peter went down in the elevator, leaving Daniels with Krakow's body. Peter ran over to the desk. "Did a woman with a scar on her face leave here a few minutes ago?"

"Miss Stanley? Yes, sir. She caught a cab right out in front."

Regan's car was around the corner. He walked with exasperating slowness. Peter wanted to tug at his arm. The car was a small black sedan. Regan got behind the wheel, Robina and Peter beside him.

"I tell you everything's okay," Regan said. "If the woman is a nut, we'll get her committed. Relax, Hume."

Robina patted the back of Peter's hand. "She'll be okay, lad."

As they rounded the corner onto the quiet street where Annaly lived, Regan pointed ahead and said, "See? There's George. Right on the job."

Suddenly he leaped closer to the windshield and squinted ahead. He gasped and the car jumped ahead. He pulled it into the curb in a screaming stop and piled out.

George was a lanky man in a tan suit and dirty white shoes. He stood on the sidewalk, rocking from side to side and making a whimpering noise like a whipped child. He held his hands cupped over his eyes.

As they ran toward him, he took his hands down, and his mouth twisted into an inverted smile, the gesture of a person trying to open eyes that are stuck together. But where his eyes should have been were pockets of torn, ragged tissue, wet with blood and fluid which ran down his lean, tan cheeks.

Robina screamed and turned her face toward Peter's jacket. Regan was cursing in a low, almost monotonous tone. The thirty-eight was in his hand as he pounded up the front steps. Robina braced herself, walked to George and took his arm.

"George," she said, "your eyes are hurt. Take it easy. I'll get you into the house and we'll phone a doctor."

"A woman," George said brokenly. "She stopped and asked me where she could find somebody whose name I couldn't catch. She was smiling. She had a scar on her face and neck. When I leaned closer to her to catch the name—she j-jabbed—and the lights went out."

PETER followed Regan into the house. The house seemed still. Too still. The silence of death. Suddenly, from upstairs, there was a choked, ragged scream.

"Come on!" Regan yelled. He took the stairs three at a time, slamming off the wall at the turn in the staircase.

At the top he paused, listened intently and then smashed his shoulder into a closed door. The frame splintered and the door crashed open. Looking beyond him, Peter saw Annaly cowering in a corner, seated on the floor, her pale hair disordered.

Lynda stood above her, holding a small kitchen knife upraised. She turned an empty face toward the door. The eyes were flakes of coal. The scar glowed red. She looked at Regan without interest as he said, "Drop it, lady!"

Ignoring the gun in Regan's hand, Peter threw himself straight at the two women. The knife drove down toward Annaly's face. His outstretched hand thrust against her wrist, deflecting the knife. It tore through Annaly's pale hair, but did not harm her.

Lynda was enormously strong with the unbelievable strength of madness. He dimly heard Regan yelling to him to stand aside. Somehow he found her wrist, held it tight. She tried to spin away from him, but he managed to retain his hold.

They rolled away from the corner, away from where Annaly was slumped in a dead faint. They both came to their feet at the same instant. Lynda yanked her hand free, drew the knife back.

In his mind it was as though the scene was suddenly taking place in slow motion. The blade was floating toward his belly and his balled fist was moving toward her jaw. Already he seemed to feel the hot, steaming pain of the thrust that would disembowel him.

The shock of the blow ran up his arm.

The point of the knife touched him, and then moved away, falling from a limp hand as Lynda spun half around and dropped on her face, her hand against Annaly's ankle.

He stood for a moment and looked down at Lynda, remembering the sultry warmth of the Calcutta nights, the more sultry warmth of her lips. . . .

Weakly he moved to the wall. He leaned against it and covered his eyes, vaguely conscious that Lynda was being bound, lifted, carried out.

Suddenly a shot crashed in another part of the house. Regan stood very still, his eyes intent, and then he seemed to crumple.

"What was that?" Peter asked.

"George. He must have figured it—I forgot to take his gun away from him."

They had taken Annaly into the next bedroom. As Regan went slowly downstairs, Peter went in to look at Annaly.

She looked up at Peter with a sort of dull anger. "You were going to pay them!" she said. "You were going to turn me into a—a drudge!"

He tried to smile. "I won't have to, now."

She looked confused. Her face brightened. She was the small girl who had been given back the ice cream cone. "Come kiss me, darling," she said.

"Were you frightened?" he asked.

"She wouldn't really have hurt me, Peter.. Not really," she said confidently.

Peter looked at her and he suddenly saw her for the first time. A small beautiful, desirable girl, with the mind of a petulant child. Not a partner—but someone to be cared for, looked after.

As from a great distance, he heard his own voice saying, "Annaly, I hope that some day you will grow up. And I hope that when you do, you will meet someone who will appreciate you."

As he left the room he heard her call plaintively. But he didn't go back. He knew that she would soon get over the damage to her pride, just as he knew that life would never actually touch her. . . .

It was after nine before all the statements had been dictated, typed and signed and before Chief Daniels felt willing to release them. Peter watched Annaly, seeing in her eyes the bright interest of one who attends an interesting movie. He wondered why he hadn't understood her before. Maybe that Cowl fellow would be willing to shoulder the burden of a child wife.

He wrote a three hundred dollar check for Regan and thanked him. Regan smiled thinly at the check and tucked it away, made no answer.

Robina left first. Peter was released a few minutes later. He hurried out, looked up the dark street in disappointment.

Then he slowed his steps, began to walk wearily home.

He walked near the big elms, his shadow revolving across the dark lawns as he passed the street lights.

"Hello, hero," the soft voice said.

He stopped and turned. She leaned against one of the huge trees, her cigarette a glowing red dot in the velvet night.

He held her wrists tightly, the cigarette making a tiny shower of sparks as it dropped into the grass. She had a woman's lips, a woman's body, a woman's strength.

There would be plenty of time later on to tell her how he had been wrong about Annaly, how it had been her all the time.

Plenty of time later.

Not right now.

Because, at the moment, Peter B. Hume, attorney at law, was kissing his secretary, and in some silent and mysterious way, they were telling each other all manner of things that could never be expressed in words.

THE END

None But the Vengeful Heart

By Bruce Cassiday

Marcy cried: "Charlie! Don't!"

♦

SUDDENLY the inside of the phone booth felt empty of air. He took a quick strangling breath, wiped his dry face with a shaking hand, and pressed the receiver to his ear.

"What did you say? *What*, Nick?"

With the last jealous beat of her poisonous heart, Charlie Young's wife would destroy the woman he loved—unless Charlie Young turned murderer.

"She beat it, Charlie. She almost tore off the door handle getting out. She beat it in the rain. I took a shot at her and—"

"You didn't hit her!" gasped Charlie Young, his face drawn up tight on one side.

"No. She ran out into the woods. I don't know where she went. I tried to stop her—"

"If anything happens to her, Nick, I'll get you! I'll get you and kill you! Now get out of town and lay low! Hear me?"

"Ease off, Charlie. I'm the guy that's doing the favor, ain't I? I think you're crazy to bother with a—"

Charlie Young didn't hear any more. He hung up the receiver and leaned back against the booth wall. He lifted a hand to his hot forehead. He pulled on the door handle and the door folded in toward him with a stabbing squeal.

Through the entrance to the roadhouse bar, Charlie Young could hear the mournful howl of wind and the stinging slash of heavy rain. A brilliant splash of blue burnt through the sky, followed briefly by a roaring crash of thunder. Charlie stood staring out into the road and he could not think straight.

Marcy had gotten away. She'd run off into the woods in the rain and neither Nick Macado nor Tony Russo had been able to stop her. So she was as good as dead.

Marcy Worth—dead. That didn't sound good. It didn't sound good at all, because it was Charlie Young's fault that she would be dead. Dark, lovely, black-haired Marcy . . . dead.

Charlie Young climbed heavily up onto the end bar stool and slumped over the counter, his coat twisted up over his heavy shoulders, one long leg folded sideways under the stool. "Joe," he said softly, "give me a rye. Forget about the water."

The thin yellow mask that was Joe Donavan's face stared at Charlie Young, looked down at the trembling big hands on the bar, glanced back to Charlie Young's tough, long face. Then he reached under the bar for a bottle.

"Sure, Mr. Young," He poured the drink in a shot glass and went back in the corner, wiped glasses, and stared from behind his face at Charlie Young, interested questions passing through his yellow eyes. . . .

The door tore open before Charlie Young could turn. He knew who it would be.

A tall, slender girl with black hair and dark eyes stumbled into the bar, her hair streaming down around her neck, her eyes wild with terror and cold, and her dress and coat soaked with water. Her skirt was torn to shreds about her long legs, and her knees were scratched from running through tangled underbrush. The smell of drenched dogwood and pine was on her.

"Oh, Charlie!" she cried, and ran over to him. Slowly he turned, and as he held out his hand to steady her, he felt her rain-smeared shoulder under his palm. An electric jolt ran up his arm and through him, and as he stared at her pale, agonized face, all the energy in him drained out in one shuddering breath.

Then she was in his arms, sobbing against his chest, her cheek laid on his shirt front, and he was holding her tightly, smoothing out her tangled, drowned hair. His eyes were focused out in the storm-torn roadway. There was a bitterness and a despair deep in them that began in his guts and ended off somewhere in the black of the dead night.

This was the woman for him, this ripe, long-limbed girl with the shining eyes and pale white face. But she would never be his; she *could* never be his. He felt her relax to him in an effortless abandonment—and his need for her made him curse more than ever the loneliness and hopelessness he would never escape.

Time began again and she got herself out of his arms and looked at him. In her eyes there was a puzzled anxiety, but no accusation. The fact that she was innocent of suspicion tore him apart completely, but he froze his face.

"It was two men," she stammered, her teeth chattering in the cold, her big fear-torn eyes staring at Charlie's hair. "They came in and asked for Joan. I—I let them in. They came into the living room and one of them grabbed my mouth and the other tied me up. I got loose in the car and jumped out."

Charlie didn't say anything. Nothing he could think of to say would pass through his paralyzed vocal cords. He took out a cigarette case and offered her a cigarette. She reached for it with trembling, soaked hands and dropped the cigarette she took out.

She looked down at it on the floor, and smiled a broken smile at Charlie. She reached for another, but her hand was shaking so much she could not pick it out. Charlie took a cigarette, lit it, and put it in her mouth. She dragged off it— a deep, heavy drag—and then with a shiver she tried to pull herself together.

"Who was it, Charlie? Who could it have been? It's terrible—things like that happening when my sister's so sick. I—I hope nothing's happened to her!"

So do I, said Charlie Young to himself, uttering the words in a sort of prayer. *I hope she never dies. I hope to heaven my wife lives forever.*

"Let's go back, Charlie! Let's get back there quick. And why are you down here at the Glen, Charlie? Why aren't you home with Joan? What are you doing?"

Charlie stared at her standing there in front of him—a wet, black-haired girl, standing straight and trim and tall, facing him with her accusing black eyes.

Then he grinned, and the grin cracked across his face like the split in a death mask. "I'm getting plastered, Marcy. I wish I could tell you why."

HE TURNED his face away from her, slid his back around. Slowly she circled the stool and looked up into his face. "Charlie," she said gently. "She's going to die?"

He tried to frame the words. But he knew he couldn't say them. How could he tell her that Joan wasn't the only one who was going to die; that Marcy as well must die too? And all because of Charlie. All because of him. . . .

He had first sensed something terribly wrong the day Doc Tanner had come to see Joan after her last attack. Doc Tanner had been one of the few around town who had been friendly to Charlie. But when he stepped out of Joan's room that day, he had stared at Charlie as if he were a live and crawling thing.

Charlie had been too astonished to challenge Tanner immediately. "How is she, doc?"

Tanner slowly drew out a huge gold winding watch from his pocket and held it in his hand. He flicked open the gold top and checked the time. Then he closed it meticulously and put it back. His deep-set eyes lifted to Charlie, and they were hard and cold and blue in his long, cadaverous face.

"Bad," he said. "Very, very bad, Young."

Young. Tanner always called him "Charlie." Charlie sat down, took out a cigarette.

"What is it?"

Tanner leaned his gaunt frame against the wall, hands in his pockets, still watching Charlie's face. "You should know, Young."

"Yeah?"

"She's dying, Young—but I guess that's no surprise to you, is it?"

Something cold and icy gripped Charlie. He could not flick the cigarette lighter. His hand hung suspended in front of his face, and he could only breathe in and out slowly. His chest seemed suddenly made of concrete. His tongue became very dry.

"What the hell do you mean?" His words were hoarse and uneven.

Tanner picked at his right ear lobe with his thumb and finger. His forehead wrinkled an instant as he relaxed, and then he was back at it, frozen and hard.

"Young, I liked you when you married Joan. I thought you'd be a steadying influence for an irresponsible play-girl. I thought you could keep her from driving herself to death."

Charlie got his cigarette lit and hid behind a screen of smoke.

Tanner's bright blue eyes were twin flicks of fire. "I made one hell of a mistake."

The cool smoke soothed Charlie's dry lungs, but there was no relaxation in his chest. His temples and neck throbbed. "Yeah?"

Tanner jangled some coins in his pocket with his hand. "Now I can see your plan clearly. It isn't a pleasant thing to think about." The blue eyes were aflame now, and they were working on Charlie's.

"Mind you, Young, I don't have many moral scruples left myself—I'm a scientist and a man of very little faith. But I do hold it a heinous crime to tamper with the lives of human beings—when they are so near death!"

"What are you trying to say, Tanner? What do you mean?" Charlie had taken two steps nearer Tanner without realizing it. His knees were rigid and his back tensed. His hands were tight and the palms itched.

"Money, Young. Money."

"Why, you—!" But Charlie caught himself even before Tanner reached out a slender hand and pushed his chest.

"I took the liberty of questioning Joan this afternoon, Charlie. About your conduct toward her. Since you've been home from the Navy you've led her a merry hell. Tennis, golf, swimming—everything she shouldn't have done, Young."

"My Lord, Tanner! She insisted on those things! Why do you think she married an athlete in the first place? I was a damned good partner in golf; I was a good companion at tennis. She made me drag her out to the links last week. I swear, Tanner, if you're insinuating—"

The expression of indifference in Tanner's icy blue eyes silenced him. "She wouldn't lie to me, Young."

"She said *I* insisted on taking her out?" The cold dread fear that had been working through Charlie's system had finally found his stomach, and his vitals were clamped into a bitter knot.

Tanner didn't say a word. His blue eyes gave the answer. He pushed himself away from the wall with a shrug of the shoulder, and then he was walking past Charlie and putting on his hat in the hallway. Charlie was too dazed to follow him out and close the door after him.

Why should she lie to me? Charlie kept repeating. Why should she lie to Tanner? Why? Why? Why? It had been Joan who had wanted to go out. Joan had said Tanner okayed a bit of exercise. Her heart was better and—But it wasn't. It was worse. And now she was almost dead.

Why, for Pete's sake, why had she lied?

DAZEDLY he led Marcy Worth to the car outside the Glen. He started the motor and backed out into the shimmering roadway. Then he roared around and headed for their house.

Beside him she huddled down, shivering a bit, pulling the heavy rug from the back seat tightly about her. She kept watching Charlie out of the corner of her eye. Finally, when she realized he was going to offer no explanation, she said:

"Charlie. You were going to tell me something. What was it?"

Charlie didn't look at her. His eyes remained on the road ahead, trying to pick out the winding white line through the slanting gray rain drowning it out.

"Something's wrong, isn't it, Charlie? Not only about Joan, but—about *us*."

Charlie gritted his teeth together. The muscles along his jaw bulged out, and Marcy saw that.

"Do you think she suspects? Do you think she knows, Charlie?" Her voice was anguished and her white face pained.

"Hell, yes, she suspects," grated out Charlie. "It's not so simple as all that. Marcy, either. You and I have done nothing. We haven't even—touched each other. I think she can just sense the feeling between us."

"It's me, Charlie. I must have let her know—just by the way I've been lately. So alive and unlike myself."

"Don't think about it. Please. There's nothing that can be done. She suspects, and she's going to do something about it. It's almost too fantastic to believe."

He turned to Marcy. "Joan has always been jealous of you, Marcy. She hates you."

Marcy's eyes went round and startled and her mouth was a red little O as she gaped at him. "Of course that isn't true! We've always been so close! Why, Joan and I—"

"No. Joan loved Harry Worth—but Harry loved you and married you. Joan wanted him, and he didn't tumble. She's hated you because of him."

"Hated me? Oh no!" whispered Marcy, staring ahead into the rain.

Charlie turned and studied her for an instant. His glance flicked back to the road again. "She was glad when Harry was killed in the war, because that left you alone. When I came along—well, you know how that happened. I was one damned lonely fool. That's all, Marcy. Except Joan's got us both now—in the most beautiful frame-up I've ever seen!"

"Frame-up?"

"She's going to die. Tanner knows. I could tell by his eyes. But that isn't all. She's written a letter about us two."

"Letter?"

"She's given Tanner a letter to open if she dies. Inside it she says she thinks you are going to poison her—feed her too many sleeping pills. She thinks you are working in conjunction with me. She thinks I'm ruining her heart so she'll become ill—a set-up for poisoning."

"No! I—I don't believe it!"

"She told me, Marcy. She wanted me to be sure to know what was going to happen to us!"

"But what does that have to do with those men tonight?"

Charlie took a deep breath. He was almost in command of himself again. "I hired them, Marcy. I knew some pretty unsavory people before I got in the Navy. I wanted to get you away from the house tonight so you'd have an alibi. They were going to keep you in a cabin in the woods. It was the only way to prove you innocent. But you got away."

Charlie was watching Marcy now, and his eyes were full on hers. She stared back at him in the dark, and there was a remote, frightened hopelessness lying deep in both of them as they gazed at each other.

"I can't leave her, even if she does hate me," said Marcy finally. She huddled deeper in the blanket, almost swallowed up in it. "I'll stick by her. She's helpless. She needs me."

Charlie stared ahead of him at the road. He could feel Marcy facing him, and as they rode along silently he could almost sense the doubt in her eyes, as if she were thinking: *maybe that's a lie; maybe those men came to kill me, too; maybe he is trying to kill both of us for our money....*

The rain was slashing flat across at them as they tore their way through it to the front door. The wind lashed the eaves mercilessly, and somewhere a broken shutter banged. Charlie Young pushed the heavy oak door shut behind him and stood there, leaning exhaustedly against it.

She faced him quietly, looking up at him in the dim orange hall light. "I'm going up to her, Charlie. She needs me. I guess maybe I'm the only one who ever understood her."

"Marcy!" called Charlie Young, but she was gone.

He found the .38 Colt right where he'd left it—in the middle drawer of the writing desk. He slipped the clip out and counted the seven slugs. He put the clip back and dropped the gun in his pants pocket. It slapped against his leg as he went up the stairs.

He didn't knock on Joan's door. He pulled it open and walked in.

Marcy wasn't there. Joan was lying on the bed, half propped up on the pillow, her face yellow in the shaded bed lamp. She was asleep now and her pale, calm face was devoid of tension or any of its usual tautness.

He walked over and stood there staring down at her. He aimed the gun and pressed the trigger—but nothing happened. Startled, he twisted the gun in his palm and checked the safety. A near smile ran over his face. He'd left the safety on.

"Charlie!" He hadn't heard the door open behind him. He whirled and looked into the terrified eyes of Marcy Worth. "Charlie! Don't! Not now!"

HE LIFTED the gun from her tearing fingers. He pulled himself away from her, aiming the Colt at Joan's chest, steadying himself against the screaming soft fury tearing with her claws and kicking with her heels and screaming with her throat.

"*Charlie! She's dead!* Anna already called Dr. Tanner. Charlie!"

His eyes traveled from Marcy's terrified face to Joan's chin, almost transparent features. *Dead.* Of course. He saw the half-filled bottle of pills on the stand. She

could have taken as many of them as she wanted. She'd beaten him again, somehow, just as she'd always managed to beat him.

He felt mad bitter laughter welling up inside him—and a mad irrepressible need to yell it to the heavens that he'd been cheated again. But downstairs a door creaked open. Charlie spun around.

"That's Doc Tanner."

Marcy stared at him, her eyes whipped. "Oh, Charlie! What can we do? We can't get out now!"

Charlie looked at the gun in his hand and then he looked at Marcy. A strange darkness filled his eyes. If he shot at Marcy—wounded her—he could clear her.

He shook his head. No one would believe that trick. A man would do that to clear an accomplice. Marcy would not be safe.

There was one way he could make an alibi for Marcy. One way— if he could manage it.

"Marcy." He moved toward her, eyes masked and hard. She saw his expression and her own eyes grew big and startled.

"I'm going to hurt you, Marcy. Hit me!"

She was backing away now, slowly, deliberately. "I—I can't hit you," she whimpered.

"You've got to!" His words choked out of his throat like animal growls. "You found me poisoning her. You tried to shoot me. I grabbed the gun and we fought."

"No, Charlie! I'm in this with you. We're together, Charlie! We'll always be together!"

She was flat against the wall now, sliding along it, trying to get away—it didn't matter where. He caught her then, held her by the neck. Her flesh turned frantic under his hand. Her pulse raced away and the artery in her neck was hot and warm beneath his palm.

"Charlie!" she whispered in a half-audible gasp.

And then all the flesh of his body and the blood in his veins turned traitor to Charlie Young. The skin that had been frantic under his palm suddenly turned to incredibly satiny flesh, and the soft mouth that was so close was crying out for his.

Charlie Young's hand slipped down from her neck along her back and found the soft flesh of her arm. He circled her to him, and her breath was warm on his face. "Charlie, Charlie."

Then his mouth was on hers, and she was pressing herself close to him. Her hands crept up his back and wandered around his ear and in the hair at the back of his head.

And the laughter welling up within him now was the laughter of exultation and triumph. In his arms was all that he had searched for so blindly all the bleak years of his life. It was in his arms, and it was his alone—and he could not have it.

From somewhere came the sound of those short, methodical footsteps climbing the stairs.

Like a man breaking barehanded through a ring of chains, Charlie Young tore away from her. He forced her out of his arms, and pulled his face from hers, holding her and looking down at her relaxed, transported face. Her mouth was open and her lips sparkled.

"Marcy! I—" But he could choke out no sound. He held her off from him then, held her soft, pliant body at arm's length. And as the steps paused outside the door, he slapped her hard on the face—first hard on one cheek and then on the other one.

She winced with pain and her eyes that had been so clear and star-strewn clouded over with terror and agony. "Charlie!" she whispered. "Please!" She grabbed onto him and tried to hide her face on his chest. "Together, Charlie."

He closed his eyes to keep the sight of her out. A cold and sickening sweat oozed out on his body, and his stomach knotted into a hard lump. He drew back his fist. He could hear the door swinging open, and a shout go up:

"Good Lord!"

He turned then, his face a mass of sweat and agony. He stared into the astonished and outraged eyes of Doc Tanner, coming at him like a gaunt bird of prey, his hands raised like claws.

He let Doc Tanner drag him from the room. He gasped out his story as best as he could: he had poisoned Joan, and Marcy Worth had seen him, tried to stop him. No one could believe Marcy Worth was helping him. . . .

"Charlie," he heard finally, a long time later. A smooth hand was at work on his twisted hair. "Charlie, it's all right."

"All right?" He turned his head to the wall. "How can it ever be all right anymore?"

Then Doc Tanner's voice came to him, low and soothing. "I checked up on your story. It was true that Joan wanted to kill herself. Others at the links heard words between you. There and at the tennis courts.

"About that letter she wrote me, Charlie. Marcy couldn't have tried to poison her sister. There wasn't a trace of sleeping pills in her body. Joan Young died before she could commit suicide. She outwitted herself."

A door closed, and then Marcy's voice came to him, soft and warm: "Charlie—I'm ashamed of you."

"I—I shouldn't have hit you, Marcy. Even to save you."

"A big strong guy like you—pulling his punches like that. Promise me you'll never do that again."

He smiled suddenly. "Okay, darling," he told her. "I promise."

The gods who made Edwina cursed her with the terrible gift of irresistible beauty—and sat back, laughing, to watch her turn men into beasts.

By Marian O'Hearn

No Deadlier Worship

**Dramatic Novelette
of a Fatal Heritage**

◆　　　◆

Tom, unseen by Edwina, took a revolver from his pocket, broke it and checked the loads. . . .

CHAPTER ONE

Birthright of Catastrophe

THE man's eyes lost their interested gleam and his feet shifted awkwardly as if wanting to turn away from her. He was a thin, shabby man, and he was suddenly miserable.

"Why do you do this?" Edwina repeated. "Why do you and all the others have to force your attentions on me?"

He took an uncertain, backward step as a policeman turned the corner. Edwina's hands flew to her face, ran destructively through her carefully curled hair, and she screamed: "Officer! Officer—help!"

The policeman shot forward, his solid feet bringing echoes from the sidewalk. The man whirled and began to run.

The policeman shouted after him, and the man skidded to a stop, his bony body seeming to crumple inside his clothing.

"Now." The husky, middle-aged cop caught his arm and hauled him around to Edwina, who was waiting with her hands over her face. "What's going on here, lady?"

She made a shuddering, sobbing sound and lowered the concealing hands. "He—" She fixed the policeman with her blue, prominent eyes. "He—" She broke off on a sob.

"I didn't mean anything." The man, who was young and cheaply dressed, looked down at the pavement, his face swollen with embarrassment. "I just—spoke to the lady. No harm intended. I thought—"

"Shut up," the cop cut him off. "You wolves never mean anything when you start annoying women. But if you're caught you whine. Maybe you'll remember this when you get another such idea."

"Yes, sir. I will. I sure will." The man continued to stare at the sidewalk in the attitude of a shamed animal.

"Then get on about your business and behave yourself. If I ever find you bothering another woman I'll take you in."

A shuddering sob once more broke from Edwina. "You don't understand, officer" she said faintly. "He—oh, I can't tell you!"

"Wait a minute, you." The policeman took a fresh grip on the man's arm. "Now lady, just what'd he do? I thought it was just a pickup try but—"

Edwina shook her head and her mouth twisted in even greater distress.

The cop's grip turned into a vise twisting the captive's flesh. "Tell me about it. Listening's my job, lady."

"I can't." The words broke but she forced herself to look up at the policeman. "Well, maybe I can explain, just to you." Flushing, hands agitated, she edged closer and spoke in a whisper.

The cop stiffened and his rosy jaws turned purple. He jerked the man forward. "So that's the kind you are! You filthy moron." And his hard, gloved fist smashed into the other's mouth.

"Listen—listen to me! I didn't mean anything—"

The fist swung again and blood spurted from the man's lower lip, jetted down his chin. He sagged, hunching his bony shoulders up toward his face, trying to ward off the blows.

Edwina's watching blue eyes glistened, and the tip of her tongue flicked across lips which were shaping into a faint smile.

"I just thought we could have a drink together."

"Shut up!" Calm returned to the law's official tone. "Let's get started. You come along now, lady, to sign the complaint."

"Complaint? Do you mean I'm to go to headquarters? Oh, I can't!"

"Just to the station. It won't take long."

"No, no, please! If my husband heard of this, I don't know what might happen! He'd want to kill him."

"No danger of that. We'll see he's safe."

"You don't understand. I just couldn't explain to my husband or—repeat anything, any part of it. I won't go with you."

"I can't arrest a man without a complaining witness, lady. I'll have to let him go."

"Then do it. And thank you, thank you, for protecting me."

The cop, released his captive and made a brief, definite gesture in the man's direction. "Get going, bum. And don't stop."

EDWINA watched him dart away, moving at a scurrying run, body still hunched and shrunken inside his cheap clothing. She pulled her glance back to the policeman, smiled, murmured another 'thank you' and walked east, toward Fifth Avenue. She walked without hurry, back straight and head high, a smile faint as a whisper on her lips.

At Fifth, a store window decorated with mirrored panels flashed a triple reception, and she paused to view the pretty woman whose clothes were intriguingly defiant of seasonal conventions.

Although the early spring day was chilly, she wore a full-skirted dress of golden yellow and a short, chalk-white coat. Her reptile platform shoes were yellow, her bag white. She was bareheaded and the mirrors showed her fair hair to be brightly sheened. "A pale nimbus around my head," she thought and the faint smile stirred her mouth, added to the glisten of her eyes. Yes, this picture *was* pretty—not that of a woman, which denoted maturity, but a girl whom life touched caressingly.

There were exceptional people, a few special people like herself who were mysteriously superior to rules and calenders. She, being of the unusual, the special, could take on the deepening beauty of living without surrendering the clarity and glow of first youth.

Her glance wavered to her throat. Frowning, she straightened and tilted her head a little higher. She must not let herself become careless about posture. No one, not even those whom Time was unable to command, could afford that.

She adjusted the collar of her short white coat and walked on. Tom was always so pleased about her youthfulness. Her smile flickered up and broadened into a crooked grin. During eight years of marriage, he had continued to look on her as the lovely girl he had courted and married.

Edwina looked at her wristwatch and began to hurry. It was five-thirty and he might be home. He hated waiting for dinner because that delayed getting back

to his books and ledgers. Whenever she objected to an office in the apartment or protested at his spending evenings there, he blinked and said he was "just about caught up with the work." And half an hour later he would be at the desk in the little room near the kitchen.

A block from the apartment house she quickened her stride and began to breathe so swiftly that her heart pounded against the wall of her chest. Clattering the key in the lock of their ground floor garden apartment, she crashed the door open. "Tom! Tom—oh, are you here?"

"Yes. In the kitchen." His voice sounded muffled, thin with weariness.

"Tom!" Leaving the front door open, she raced through the living room to the hall.

"What is it, Edwina? What's happened?" Tom was grotesque in one of her aprons, with his head thrust forward as he stared through thick-lensed glasses.

"You're here! I got back all right— and you're here. Hold me. Hold me tight!"

She plunged at him, letting her handbag drop. She threw both arms around him, bent her head because of the slight difference in height and clung to him.

"Eddie, Eddie. Sit down here in this chair. That's it. Rest while I get you a drink of water. Lean back and close your eyes."

He brought the water, slopping it over the rim of the glass as he held it to her lips. Finally, in spite of the tears choking her words, she was able to talk.

"This man—I don't know how long he'd been following me. I first noticed him when I came out of the drugstore. He tipped his hat and said something, so I began to hurry. He kept right after me and started to overtake me. I was terrified then, but at the last corner he ran up and caught hold of me, held onto my arm and wouldn't let me go."

Tom Baldwin patted her shoulder reassuringly. "Why didn't you scream or call for a policeman?"

"I don't know. Maybe I did scream. But there weren't any police around. Not in sight, anyhow. So he held onto me, right there on the sidewalk and said: "Tell me who you are. I've got to know so I can find you again. You're so beautiful. So young and lovely.' I managed, finally, to break free and ran the rest of the way home. Oh, Tom. . . . " She sagged against him, shuddering.

"POOR girl," he murmured in his fatigue-muffled voice. "You'd better not talk about it any more. Lie down and I'll finish dinner. Come on, sweet, I'll put you to bed."

"Aren't you going out and look for him? Maybe he's near, waiting!"

"Not much chance of that. He'd leave, fast, when he realized this was your home. Please lie down, Eddie.". He led her into the bedroom, helped her off with her dress, removed the silk bedspread. "I'll call you when dinner's ready."

"Be sure the front door's locked. I don't think I even closed it."

He went out, walking softly, and she heard him moving about the apartment, latching the front door, returning to the kitchen.

She pulled a second pillow under her head, slid her shoulders up against it and looked around the room, letting her lashes veil the blue prominence of her eyes. The corners of her lips flickered and she thrust aside the light blanket Tom had spread over her. Getting out of bed, she slipped on her prettiest negligee, went to the window and glanced through the venetian blind.

Yes, he was there again, as he had been every day at this time for almost a week. Sitting at the window, smoking and looking down into the courtyard. Dark, thick hair; a masculine slant to his jaw. He was young and, she was sure,

tall. She liked the fact that he smoked a pipe.

She closed the blind, looked down at the white, lace-frothed negligee which fell open softly to reveal her silk-clad knees. Reaching for the cords controling the blind, she rolled it up and bent her head in the open window as if studying the flower strips in the garden.

He was watching her, seeing a slim, graciously feminine girl dreaming over blossoms which could not match her own loveliness. The light at this angle must be making a soft pale nimbus of her hair as, unconscious of being observed, she appeared before him in the sheer robe.

"Eddie?" Tom's voice was gentle and anxious but it startled her away from the window. She had not heard the door open or sensed his presence until he was peering in at her, head thrust forward, eyes straining behind the thick lenses. "You're not sleeping? Dinner's ready if you feel like eating."

She followed him out to the kitchen dinette. As she ate, she thought of the dark head framed in the second-floor window. His hair was so black. He was youthfully lean, too. High cheek bones with the faint suggestion of shadows under them. A nice, man's mouth.

Tom helped her clear away and asked: "Feel all right now? If you do, I've got some work to finish. It won't take long."

Her lips settled and pressed against each other. "Again?" she demanded. "You're going to spend another evening in that room scribbling figures? You're going to—" She broke off and began to stack the soiled dishes in the sink.

"It's important, Eddie. We're shorthanded at the office and I've got to be ready for the annual audit."

She continued to clatter dishes, keeping her back toward him until she felt him leave, heard him enter the room which held his world of ledgers.

The black-haired man with the odd,

interesting shadows beneath his cheek bones might still be at his window, hoping she would return. She left the kitchen and returned to the bedroom. Rolling down the blind without glancing up at the second floor, she inspected her face and began to smile, faintly, as she made up. A little more rouge for night, heavier mascara, the blue eye shadow and the new lightning-red lipstick.

She worked slowly and contentedly, thinking of the strange, cheaply dressed man who had approached her so awkwardly. The cop's fist had made a dull, crushing sound as it smashed into his face, and the blood trickling from his lip had made a scarlet line from chin to throat. Her smile widened and she nodded at the glass, pleased with what she saw. Then she brushed her hair, shaping it into soft curls.

Her hair was strikingly attractive tonight; she must be sure never to omit the weekly visit to Miss Anges' Salon. Miss Anges herself had agreed it was ridiculous to let the climate darken hair such as hers. Some women's hair lost color with the years but that was another matter. It would be a very, very long time before she had to accept such a condition.

Touching her wrists and throat with perfume, she went to the closet and got out a long, cleverly draped gown of ice blue that was even lovelier than her white negligee. Edwina called it her "dreaming robe." And as she went with a deliberately sensuous step into the living room, she was already arranging the dreams.

CHAPTER TWO

Watcher in the Dark

THE living room, long and gracefully proportioned, was in darkness; the curtained glass doors leading into the courtyard were tightly closed.

Edwina opened them and gauzy, early moonlight caught the blue gleam of her robe. She paused in contemplation of the little fountain encircled by flowers, the towering skyscrapers that were a great, protective wall shutting out the dark rush of the city.

She had insisted on renting the apartment as soon as she saw the strangely secretive little garden. It did not matter that the doors of other apartments opened onto the courtyard shared by all the ground-floor tenants, because she had never admitted their existence.

Her glance lifted to the second floor and dropped as quickly. He was not there. His window was closed and dark. She turned into the living room, crossed to an ivory-toned reading lamp and, placing it so that only a reflected glow would touch the piano, turned on the light.

Again her glance slid to the doors. She sat down at the small grand which had been a birthday gift from Tom. As her hands touched the keys she watched them approvingly, knowing they were beautiful as music. Perhaps even more beautiful, because they were the instruments which expressed it.

Closing her eyes, she launched into Massenet, smiling as her fingers called *Thaïs* to life. As she created *Thaïs*. And then she began to create something more; something which ran stirringly through the portrait of the great, catastrophic siren. The magnificent counter theme which was herself, Edwina. Underlying the music at first, it grew until it blended with and finally dimmed out *Thaïs*. . . .

Minutes later, she opened her eyes again and became conscious of every detail of the room, every quality of her own person. The mellow shadows, the gauzy moonlight, the gleaming robe enriching her own grace.

She stopped playing, let her hands drift across the keys and turned to face the open glass doors. Had something, someone moved just outside? Her lips shaping into the suggestion of a smile, she left the piano and went toward the courtyard again, her gaze dreamily unseeing. With the lampglow outlining her, she hesitated in the doorway, sighed as she lifted her face to the far sky.

There was a tall shadow against the wall. A shadow shaped like a man. She turned into the room again and her darting glance saw that the shadow was stirring, moving to a point from which she could be seen, watched. . . .

With the air of a woman completely alone and secure from observation, she sat down and took off her high-heeled mules. Letting them fall to the floor, she zipped open her robe and pulled it over her shoulders. As she stepped out of it, clad only in a fragile slip, she looked briefly toward the tall shadow, and the tip of her tongue flicked over the dry edges of her lips.

Picking up the gown, she once more moved to the doors, as if for a last glimpse of the garden. The shadow had left the wall and become a tall man whose hair was black even in the moonlight.

Edwina left the room abruptly—but closed the door into the hall before crying: "Tom! For heaven's sake, Tom!"

There was no answer. She ran for the office, her cry lifting into a scream. "Tom! Do something quick."

She tore the door open, and her husband's misty eyes peered up through thick lenses.

"What is it, dear?" he murmured vaguely. And then, gathering himself, he got up from the desk. "What's the matter, Eddie? Tell me!"

Edwina straightened and her lips closed, hate screaming silently through her. He was such a poor thing! Without form or strength or decision. His hair was fairish but not quite blond; he was a little under average height and his pudgy body just missed plumpness. And,

of course, he earned a salary that was slightly inadequate.

"There's someone in the courtyard." Her voice broke down to a whisper. "A man—looking in at me! Watching me! I'd just slipped off my robe when I saw him."

Tom Baldwin unhooked his glases and rubbed his eyes. "You should have undressed in the bedroom," he mumbled. "Naturally other tenants might be in the garden."

Edwina made her back very straight and her head high. Her blue, prominent eyes became even wider.

"Didn't you hear what I said? There's a man out there, staring at your wife, spying on her while she's dressing. And it isn't the first time. I haven't wanted to bother you, but the same man sneaks into the courtyard every night. Sometimes he looks into the living room and at other times tries to peep through the bedroom windows. Last night, when you stayed late at the office, the blinds were open and I saw him. . . . I'm frightened, Tom."

Tom Baldwin blinked, but his face changed until the flesh tightened and his forehead ridged with anger. "Well, he won't show up again, whoever he is! When I get through with him—" The ridge on his forehead reddened and he rushed for the door.

"Wait." Edwina ran after him. "He looked big—huge. Don't go out there without protection, without a weapon of some kind!"

HER husband paused, blinked, and charged back down the hall. When he returned there was a hammer in his hand, and the ridge on his forehead was a fierce crimson.

He brushed past Edwina. When she reached the living room he was in the courtyard, shouting: "You there, what're you doing? Get out!"

"Say, fella." The answering voice was startled. "I live in this apartment house, too."

"Shut up!" Tom rushed at him. The other man backed hastily away. He was even younger than Edwina had thought. And he was tall and lean, his hair richly dark.

"Is this a gag?" he protested, still retreating. "I just came down to the garden—"

"Get out! Get out!" Tom's voice soared crazily and cracked into a falsetto scream. He gathered his pudgy body in a sudden, terrible effort and leaped.

The tall, dark youth halted, looked down at him and crouched. "Cut it out. I can take care of you with one hand—"

But he had not seen the swinging hammer. It came down at the second he crouched, striking with a crunching dull sound much like the report of the policeman's fist smashing into another man's face.

The hammer lifted again and again, crazily, and the youth, mouth open in surprise, slipped to his knees, toppled over and lay on his back.

There was a raw, gusty sound beating through the courtyard. Tom Balwin's straining, gasping breathing. He stood over the crumpled figure on the garden walk, the hammer dangling from his hand as if he had forgotten it.

Edwina moved closer. A bright line of color was seeping from the unconscious man's dark hair, jetting down his forehead. The shadows under his high cheek bones were sharp and his mouth boyish.

Her tongue tip flicked at the edge of her dry lips and she straightened. "What'll we do?" she murmured, her blue eyes still fixed on the still face. "He's right outside our door. He'll be found."

Tom's head thrust forward and his eyes were mistier than ever. The flesh of his face sagged until there was a drooping roll beneath his chin. His body sagged, too, lumping into pudgy insignificance.

"We'll have to call the police. Tell them what happened. He—he was trying to break into our apartment. Yes, we'll say that."

"If he's dead, they won't believe it. They'll ask you to prove he entered the apartment."

"Then we'll tell the truth." Tom knelt, peered into the unconscious man's half-open eyes. "He's not dead, thank God. Go inside and telephone the police, Edwina."

"No." She bent and put a hand on his shoulder, clenched her fingers into the flesh. "They'll ask questions, take us up to the police station. And if it gets into the papers. . . . People won't pay any attention to the facts—they'll say all sorts of things. The police will ask me things no woman should have to answer! Tom, you can't do that to me, to your wife."

Tom pushed himself laboriously to his feet, noticed the hammer and dropped it with a convulsive gesture. "Do you want to leave him here? When he's found, the police'll take charge anyhow."

"No—no." Her glance touched the dark hair and the bright line of blood which was spreading along one brow toward the temple. "Listen. . . ." She dropped her voice to a whisper and touched her lips with her tongue. "We'll carry him through the courtyard to the alley behind. Leave him there. If he's found, we don't know anything about it, any more than anyone else in the building. Why should they connect us with—what happened to him?

Baldwin's eyes seemed all mist. Horrible, straining, peering mist. The new, soft roll of flesh under his chin was trembling. "He needs a doctor, medical attention. He's—I didn't mean to hit him so often. That hammer—"

"Never mind," Edwina cut it. "It's done. And if we don't hurry someone'll see us." She looked swiftly around the doors lining the garden, up at the rows of windows above them. The doors were still closed and the windows empty. "Do as I say! You lift his shoulders, I'll take his feet."

"But this is wrong—crazy!"

"Tom, get hold of him!"

Baldwin's formless shoulders bent and he lifted the unconscious man. Edwina, her hands steady, supported the long legs. Keeping close to the building, they started for the door-like gate which led to the alley.

Once through the gate, Edwina dropped her part of the burden. "Put him down here. It's good enough. Hurry."

Turning back, she glanced around the courtyard and up at the windows. As her husband closed the gate, she put her arm through his. "If anyone sees us, they'll think we're out here for a breath of air."

Moving at a leisurely stride, her back straight and head lifted, she was irritated by the spasmodic trembling of Tom's flesh. Near the little fountain she paused and, keeping a hand on his arm, bent dreamily over the flowers.

Baldwin jerked free and stumbled into the apartment. When she followed a minute later, he had returned to the office and closed the door.

"Good night," she called, turning away with the whisper of a smile shaping her lips.

EDWINA sat up in the darkness, and the noise stabbed through her senses again. She had not been dreaming. The hoarse, crazed sounds were real.

"Tom." She reached for the other twin bed but her hand encountered only the covers, still smooth and undisturbed. The bed was empty.

She groped for the table light, switched it on. Tom had not gone to bed at all. He was still up at two o'clock. The thick, nerve-cracking noise grew worse.

She stepped cautiously into the hall and stopped to listen. Her gaze swung to the office door, fixed on it. Against her will she began to inch toward it. Her fingers were wet when they clamped on the doorknob and finally laboriously turned it.

Tom was slumped back in the desk chair, head lolling and eyes fixed. The hoarse, crazed animal sounds were coming from his open mouth.

The nameless fear went out of her and her lips clamped into scar-like whiteness. She caught his shoulders and shook him. He did not awaken. She lifted his head and held it between her hands, but his unfocused eyes did not see her.

Edwina recoiled and fled for the telephone at the end of the hall. Dr. Bickston's number was on the memo pad and she dialed it frantically. For minutes there was no answer, just a far, defeated buzzing. At last the buzzing broke and a tired voice said: "Dr. Bickston speaking."

She explained hurriedly, her words fluttering with each breath until the physician cut in soothingly. "Put him to bed and keep him warm. I'll be right over."

Edwina remained before the telephone for a moment, staring at its dull metal surface. There was nothing she could do until the doctor arrived. "Nothing," she thought. "I must stay calm. Not let this *mark* me."

Going into the bedroom, she put on the blue satin robe and made up her face. As she finished, the doorbell rang.

"Oh, doctor. I'm so glad you're here! It's—"

"Where is he?"

Her lips moved unsteadily but she forced them into a faint smile and led the way to the office, walking with straight-backed dignity, the blue robe trailing gracefully after her.

The physician put down his bag and bent over Tom. "I'll call you if I need you, Mrs. Baldwin," he said without looking at her.

"I'll be waiting right outside."

Standing within inches of the closed door, Edwina listened. The silence was disturbing, and she pressed tightly against the door, straining to hear the doctor's words. She could catch only a low murmur. At last Bickston appeared, half-leading, half-carrying Tom Baldwin.

"I'll put him to bed," he told her. "Just keep blankets over him. What he needs is immediate complete rest. I'll talk to you in a moment, Mrs. Baldwin."

She paced from hall to living room. When Dr. Bickston entered, she was standing before the closed, curtained doors to the courtyard.

"Tell me!" Her hands lifted but dropped again, and she forced a faint, determined smile over her lips. "Sorry," she said softly. "I didn't mean to be impatient."

Bickston's gray, clear glance moved over her face. He walked away from her, turned sharply back. "Something of this sort was what I feared," he said, his words precise and professional. "I didn't think it would take—quite this form, but I'm not really surprised."

Edwina's eyes widened and again her hands made that half-gesture of appeal. "I don't understand! You *expected* Tom to—become ill?"

"He's been ill for some time. Obviously you don't know that he came to see me a week ago. He wasn't sleeping well, felt too jumpy and occasionally his eyes seemed unable to focus."

"No! No, he didn't tell me. Oh, poor Tom. He probably didn't want to worry me."

Bickston cleared his throat. "I warned him, then, he'd have to slow up, get rid of nervous tension. It appeared to be something more than overwork, although that was part of it. My guess was that he was under some emotional strain."

"But can't something be done to help him get well?"

"Maybe. If the strain could be ended, or at least eased. That's part of your job for the next few days, Mrs. Baldwin. Try to make him relax and see that there are no shocks, no irritations, nothing to upset him."

"Then this is—serious?"

"Maybe. I'll know more about it tomorrow. Call me in the morning and I'll arrange to drop in during the day. I've given him a shot and he'll sleep for some hours."

"The way he was acting, though, as if—"

"Nerve collapse does strange things. Good night now. Let me hear from you tomorrow."

He was gone, clicking the door neatly behind him. He was a machine, a dry bloodness machine stamping out medical opinions. Meaningless as a man.

She remembered a slanting masculine chin and shadows under high check bones. The thin, shining red line of blood had seeped from his black hair onto his forehead. And now he was lying in the alley, unless. . . . Suppose he had been discovered, regained consciousness and named his assailant?

Her tongue flicked over her lips and she moved to the glass doors. pushed them slowly open. Closing them as carefully, she went along the garden path to the gate.

Had anyone heard Tom's weird, startling outbreak? The crazed animal-like noises which had come from their apartment in the middle of the night? If they had they would remember, later. And if the dark-haired man died, Dr. Bickston would testify as to Tom's mental condition, could state that she had called him after her husband's terrifying seizure had awakened her.

Her tongue tip touched her lips and she opened the gate. The alley was empty. And not even a tracing in the dust indicated where a tall, crumpled body might have lain.

CHAPTER THREE

The Great Theme of Edwina

"EDDIE, wake up." The voice was muffled and thin. "I've made coffee and left it on the stove. We overslept so I can't wait for breakfast."

Tom. Why was he bothering her? Didn't he always make coffee?

Tom! Her eyes opened and she started from the bed with a sense of nightmare. But he was standing beside her, his eyes misty behind the thick lenses, his head thrust anxiously forward. Last night. . . .

She wet her lips. "Dr. Bickston said you were to stay in bed. You're sick and he's coming back today."

"I can't. This is one morning I've got to get to the office. Besides, I'm feeling all right." His lips moved jerkily over his words and his face seemed swollen.

"Eddie," he sat down on the edge of the other twin bed, "I went out to the alley as soon as I woke up. There was nothing there. Do you suppose—" He broke off and his eyes changed from mistiness into glazed brightness.

Edwina hesitated, watching the glaze behind the thick lenses. "I don't suppose anything, Tom. Nothing happened, nothing at all. That man came to and left."

"Maybe not. Someone might have found him. If he did come to while he was alone, he probably called the police. If he's badly hurt, they'll wonder why we—left him there to die."

She slid her feet to the floor. "That's ridiculous. Now, will you please go to bed? I promised to call the doctor this morning."

"No." He walked to the clothes closet and took down his hat. Then he swung around to face her.

"Don't leave the apartment today. You've got to promise you won't. If you need anything, telephone. And if—something happens, call me at the office."

"Not go out? You want to me to stay inside all day?"

"Yes." His eyes, with their feverish glaze, moved from side to side. "Promise me, Eddie. Give me your promise you'll stay in and keep the door to the courtyard locked."

Edwina's eyes opened widely. She moved to the dressing table. The deep rose tone of her nightgown made her skin glow, and its long lines stressed the grace of her body. Her glance strayed to the side-view mirror and she pulled in her breath sharply, watching her waistline until the suspicion of a bulge disappeared.

"I'm waiting." Tom's voice sounded thicker and heavier. She looked at him in the glass and let her shoulders droop in a gesture of helpless surrender.

"If you're going to insist, then I'll promise." Her hands went up to her face and pressed against her eyes. Her voice roughened with tears. "It isn't fair! Other women go where they please and never worry, never suffer any—unpleasantness. It's not my fault I'm not safe on the streets."

"I know, dear." He came up to her, put his hands on her shoulders. "It's just for today, for a little while. Things will change. . . ." His face had suddenly tightened; the reddish stain was appearing on his forehead.

She turned into his arms. "I can't understand it. I try to be so careful when I'm out. Even when a man's staring at me, I pretend I don't notice. Tom, please tell me it's not something wrong in me—that it's not my fault."

The scarlet patch on his forehead swelled. "Of course it's not your fault!

You're to stop talking that way. I'll find a way to change things—you'll see. . . . Now I've got to leave. Keep the doors locked." He kissed her good-by and left.

After he had gone, Edwina drank some of the coffee he had prepared and, still in her nightgown, went through the apartment, rolling up the blinds to let in the sun. In the living room she sat at the piano and fingered a few chords of *Thaïs*, but the catastrophic, dark grandeur was missing.

She showered and put on a short frock of summer green, dull red shoes, tied a green ribbon around her hair. She was unlocking the glass doors into the courtyard when the telephone rang. It was Tom.

"Has anything happened? Anyone come? Are you all right?" His voice was thick and hoarse.

"Yes, certainly I'm all right. Nothing's happened. I'll call you if it does."

Returning to the glass doors, she opened them and stepped into the courtyard where she strolled along the path. After she had circled the fountain three times, she walked, even more casually, to the gate.

The alley was empty and silent, looking as if the night before had never happened.

Back in the apartment she paced through the rooms. It had happened. She knew it did. Tom had sprung at the tall, black-haired young man. The hammer had made a dull, crunching sound, and then the man was lying on the walk. She could even recall the weight of his long legs as she had helped carry him through the gate.

THE telephone whirred again. And again Tom Baldwin demanded to know if everything was all right.

"Don't worry," she told him wearily. "I'm staying in—if that's what you're checking on."

"Please, Eddie! You know I trust you. After you gave your promise—"

She put the phone down to cut off his protests. The day turned into marching emptiness. At two, she made another trip to her dressing table to retouch her make-up and brush her hair. As she was arranging the bright green ribbon, the sudden clatter of the telephone startled her.

"Yes," she said, picking it up. "Everything is still the same!"

"Is this Mrs. Baldwin?" It was Dr. Bickston. "I've been expecting you to call. How is your husband?"

"I'm sorry, doctor. I should've called. Tom was completely recovered this morning."

"*Recovered?*" The physician's voice was startled. "What do you mean?"

"He's not here. He went to the office."

"Went *where?*" The question ended in a smothered exclamation. "Where is his office? Give me the address."

"Why, if you wish. But what reason—"

"Just give it to me, please."

Edwina's lips pressed together. "Certainly," she murmured, each syllable edged. "It's at 2020 High Street—the phone number is Lewelyn 2-4994."

He repeated it and hung up without a good-by.

At sunset, she closed the doors into the courtyard, stared around the room. She had seen the black-haired man fall as surely as she had seen the cop's fist smash into that other man's face and bring blood spurting from his mouth.

Perhaps he hadn't been really injured —just stunned. He must have recovered soon after they had left him in the alley, and decided not to raise a fuss over what had happened. After all, he had been in the wrong. . . .

"He may be upstairs now, waiting to see me again, hoping for even a glimpse of me."

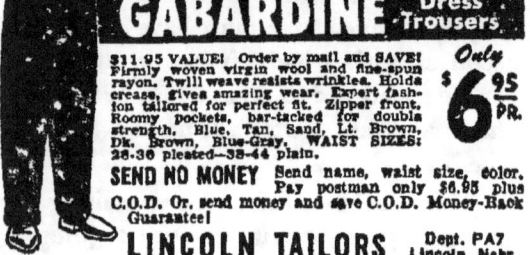
The faint smile spread her lips as she arranged a lamp so that it would touch the piano with reflected glow. She sat at the grand and began playing. The doors were still closed but the blinds were rolled up, revealing the entire scene.

Her hands moved into *Thaïs* and she watched them approvingly, closed her eyes while they began to weave the other, deeper portrait which was Edwina.

The telephone's jangle aroused her and shattered the dark grandeur she was creating.

"Eddie." Tom's voice sounded higher and so rasping that she did not recognize it at once. "I'll be late—got something to do. Don't wait dinner for me. And keep the doors closed, hear me?"

"Where are you? At the office?"

"No, haven't been there all afternoon. Doing something important. 'By.'"

The connection clicked off before the could tell him Dr. Bickston had wanted to see him. But it didn't really matter. . . .

Shadows were crowding around the lamp glow. The courtyard was dark, and she knew that it was empty. On a sudden whim, she went into the bedroom, slipped into a sapphire evening gown. If she couldn't go out, at least she could dress up at home. And the brilliant blue did wonderful things for her eyes, for her golden hair, setting off the soft white gleam of her lovely bare shoulders.

She went back to the piano and let her hands rest on the keys. She did not play, but a smile edged her lips. She wouldn't stay home tomorrow, no matter what Tom might say.

The apartment door opened with a hurried clatter as if someone had lunged against it as he turned the key. "Eddie. Eddie!"

Tom Baldwin's voice was still a strange, uncontrolled mixture of rasping determination and uncertainty. He came into the living room without removing his hat and looked at her silently. Then, noticing the rolled up blinds, he rushed at them, muttering as he jerked them down.

"Don't turn on the lights when the windows aren't covered! Anyone could be looking in at you!"

Edwina's blue eyes glistened and her lips pressed into dry whiteness. She stared at him with fury shrieking through her.

"Isn't it bad enough that I'm a prisoner here on your orders? I've been locked in, caged in all day. Now you want to keep every shade closed so that I'll really feel the prison walls!"

She stopped as she saw the tightening of his face, the reddening stain on his forehead. Letting her head droop, she went on in slow, tear-choked words:

"I might as well be dead—I can't go on living this way. Other women are free to move around, walk on the streets, go to restaurants and theaters. If men notice them at all it's just—casually. But the moment I go out, they seem to turn into beasts!"

He smiled a little, and his voice was taut with excitement. "We're going to change that, dear. I decided how to do it this afternoon. Come on, we're going out!"

"Going out? Where?"

"Never mind. Just do as I say." And he smiled, the shape of his mouth as strange as his voice. "Hurry."

"I'll have to change."

"You look all right. Just put on a coat." His hands were still in his pockets and he was leaning forward, his eyes taking on a feverish glaze.

"Well . . . all right."

She took her short, chalk-white coat from the closet, paused before the mirror to apply lipstick. Tom, unseen by Edwina, took a revolver from his pocket, broke it and checked the loads. He said impatiently: "Let's get going. This isn't a party."

"Then what is it?"

"You'll find out." He reached for her arm, hurried her through the living room to the front door and out to the street, where he hailed a cab.

"Drive down Broadway," he told the driver. Hands thrust into his pockets again, he turned to peer through the window at the thickening crowds. Near Fiftieth, he called: "Let us out here."

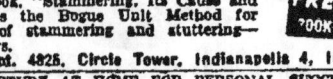

HE DROPPED a bill into the cabbie's hand and helped Edwina to the sidewalk, keeping one hand in his pocket. "Now," he said as hurrying men and women brushed past them. "You start walking—alone."

"Alone? Where are you going?"

"I'll be right behind you. See this?" The hand edged up from his pocket and the street lights glinted on the barrel of his revolver. "Got it today. After I've given a few of these birds a lesson, the others will let you alone."

She stiffened. Chill touched her, froze her mouth into shapelessness, but only for a fleeting moment. Then she was warm again, warmer than she had ever been. The cop's fist smashing into a man's mouth, sending a jet of blood from his chin. The black-haired youth crumpling to the garden walk with a scarlet line seeping across his brow. It was like great music. Like the epic of *Thaïs*. . . .

"Yes," she said, and her eyes glistened with the reflection of the glaze in his. "If that's what you want."

He nodded and she turned away, her head high. Slowly, with a deliberate sinuousness, she began walking. As her glance struck into the approving stream and heads turned toward her, the new warmth within her grew. She moved in time to the great, catastrophic theme of irresistible woman, and the faint, secret smile of knowledge edged her lips.

As she approached the corner, the

crowd was even denser. Masculine eyes rested on her, masculine mouths smiled. A stop light halted the pedestrians, and a tall, middle-aged man standing on the curb looked at her sharply. She met his glance and let her smile grow.

He inspected her even more sharply, hesitated and lifted his hat. "Good evening," he murmured in vague, polite tones.

"You!" Tom Baldwin's voice screamed above the noise of the crowd. "You're another of 'em! Another one that won't let her alone. But you will now!"

There was a barking sound, sharper than the backfiring of an exhaust. The middle-aged man's face went blank and he swayed. A woman screamed and then the swaying man fell.

The woman screamed again and other voices began to shriek hysterically. Men yelled and shoved, fighting a way through the crowd, clawing for escape.

Someone plunged into Edwina, almost knocking her down. And then the crowd was a huge, live thing behind her, driving her forward, carrying her before it. She was swept on to the next corner, past it. There the crowd dissolved, dropping her under the blazing lights of a drugstore.

She pressed close to the building and stared down the street toward the point where the man had fallen. But there was an impenetrable wall of people shutting off all view and eliminating any chance getting back to Tom.

Mounted police were galloping their horses along the street, stopping traffic and keeping the crowd on the sidewalks. A squad car, siren howling, flashed past and was followed by two others. Finally there came the mournful warning of an ambulance. .

"I'll go home," Edwina decided. "Yes, I can go home now."

* * *

Majestic darkness poured from the piano keys under Edwina's hands. Ardor

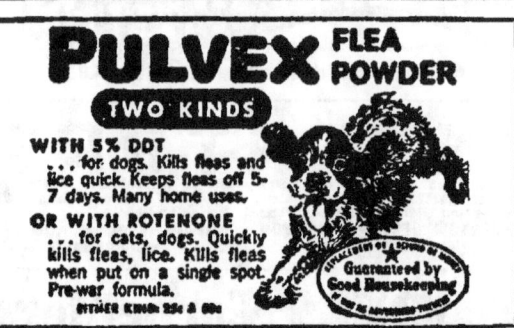

and danger, violence and death. Yet life continuing with an even greater purpose. . . .

A firm, steady buzzing cut through the music and her hands paused, her eyes opened. The doorbell.

She went to answer, her stride deliberate, sinuously rhythmic.

"Yes?" Her eyes repeated the question as she looked up at the two men standing outside the door.

"Homicide Bureau. You Mrs. Tom Baldwin?"

"Yes."

The detective stared at her under the brim of the hat he had not bothered to remove.

"Were you with your husband tonight when he shot and killed a man near Fiftieth and Broadway?"

Edwina straightened, lifted her hands and let them drop. Her eyes widened and misted with tears. "Yes." Her throat worked visibly over the word.

"Hmmm! Get dressed. We're taking you downtown."

Again the swift appeal of lifting hands and the equally swift checking of the gesture. "Downtown? To police headquarters? Am I being arrested?"

"No, but you're going to be questioned. Your husband committed murder. You witnessed it. Please hurry, lady. We'll wait here."

Edwina's blue robe trailed gracefully after her as she left the room.

The detective eyed his partner and whistled soundlessly. "What do you know about that, Jim?" he murmured. "Her husband killed this guy because he was insanely jealous of her—a faded middle-aged doll like that."

"Yeah." Jim shook his head in bewildered agreement. "A figure like a sack of meal, a face as worn out as an old calendar and bleached hair to boot!"

THE END

www.ingramcontent.com/pod-product-compliance
Lightning Source LLC
Chambersburg PA
CBHW080915020726
47502CB00008B/2458